# THE FORGOTTEN MINE

## J. ALSPAUGH

# DEDICATION

This book is dedicated to those who have not
forgotten the incredible value of every child.

# Chapter 1

I looked down the table at the man they told me was my grandfather and wondered why I had never seen him before. In fact, I had never even heard of him three days ago. He was a sturdy man with a white drooping mustache and no beard. His hair and thick eyebrows matched his mustache.

He had made no effort to engage me in conversation during the meal. But then, I hadn't either. The table was one of those long, old fashioned antique pieces made out of rich dark wood that you see in medieval movies about knights. Only my grandfather, if that was really who he was, was no knight, and I was definitely not a princess. Just a kid being shuffled between relatives while my mom tried to sort out her life.

I sighed without realizing it and leaned my head on my hand. The butler who brought the food to us was standing ready by the door that led to the kitchen. He cleared his throat softly. I lifted my head to see what it meant. He had been absolutely silent until this point. He was looking at me and his eyes darted briefly towards the white haired stranger at the other end of the table. I followed his cue and found my grandfather staring at me in disapproval. I blushed, taking my elbow from the smooth, polished wood of the table.

Grandfather murmured something that sounded like a grumble, and the butler came forward to take the plates away. I had never seen a real live butler. Only the ones on old movies. I sat back, unsure of what would happen next. I was unbelievably tired, and my head felt like it weighed a ton. Now and then, my head jerked downward as if it would fall right into my lap. I leaned back in my chair, careful not to slouch, and rested my head against the thick cushioned back.

"Porter will show you to your room. You are to remain there until you are summoned for breakfast," Grandfather said in his low voice. He looked me over and added, "Don't be late. I don't imagine a little girl like you would enjoy missing breakfast."

I couldn't help the tiny smile that played for a moment at the edges of my mouth. I was eleven, not especially tall, but definitely not a little girl. "What time is breakfast?" I asked when he said no more.

"Children are to be seen and not heard." He said it without bothering to look at me.

"Well, how can I not miss breakfast if I don't know when it is?" I asked, disregarding his quote. When he did not answer, I added, "Unless you would like me to show up in my pajamas."

He looked shocked and angry at my overly polite response. I didn't actually have pajamas with me. The transfer to his house had been a last minute switch, and my uncle forgot to get my suitcase out of his trunk before he drove away. All I had was the backpack that sat beside my chair. It was lucky for me that we had arrived when we did, or I probably would have had to go to bed hungry.

"You will be called when you are wanted," Grandfather sputtered trying to regain control.

"So I just sit there by the door all night in my clothes and shoes waiting to be called so I don't have to starve?" I asked, the politeness was wearing thin. I was tired, but more than that, I was tired of this whole endless shuffle. In three months I had lived with an unmarried aunt, a cousin, two different grandmothers, and an uncle. Most of whom I'm fairly certain were not actually relatives at all. Mom had to tell the court I was staying with family so I wouldn't get put into the system. The worst part was not knowing why this all started. Why was I being shuffled around in the first place? Mom had visited me once at the aunt's house, and she seemed well and happy enough.

"Young Lady, are you listening?" Grandfather's voice jarred me from my tired thoughts.

"I'm sorry. I did not hear what you said. Would you mind repeating it?" I was trying to be good. Mom had said, "Be good for them, Polly, and I'll come back for you." I really was trying, but there's only so much an eleven-year-old can stand.

"I said that breakfast is at 7:30. Now go to your room."

I could tell it irritated him to have to repeat himself and resolved to listen better in the future. After all, there was the secret mine on his property, and I wanted to find out where it was. I stood and picked up my backpack. All my worldly goods in one bag. I wished I had known. I would have packed differently. It didn't matter. There hadn't been time anyway.

Pulling the bag onto my shoulder, I followed the silent butler man out through the door I had entered by. I knew I would have to keep track of all the doors and halls if I was going to be there for more than a day or two. I had heard my uncle on the phone the night we left his place. He was shouting about having done his duty and that there were no more relatives however distant who would take me. He was talking to my Mom, but I had not bothered to ask if I could talk to her. They were both upset, so I stayed out of his way.

The wide, elegant entrance was dimly lit. I looked up. There were lights overhead, but they were not on.

"Why don't you turn on the lights? Can grandfather not afford the electricity?" I asked my guide.

He turned his head towards me slightly, and I saw the

evidence of a fading smile. "He prefers the authentic lighting that belongs to the house's era."

"Oh."

We turned right and started down a dim hall. I looked at the old pictures of men and women in strange flowing clothes that lined the walls. Only a few of the painted faces were smiling. "Are these his other relatives?"

Again the quick smile caused the man's cheekbones to rise. "No, they are costly pieces of art." He slowed a little and looked down at me. "It would be best if you did not touch any of them."

"My class at school, not the last school but two before that one, went to a museum for a field trip." I informed him. "We learned all about how to treat pieces of art and how expensive it can be. You don't have to worry about me touching any of them."

He nodded, "You are a smart young lady." Again his steps slowed to match my meandering pace.

"My name is Polly." I didn't know if it would matter. One of the grandmothers had called me Patricia for a whole week, even though I reminded her my name was Polly almost every day.

"It is nice to meet you, Polly."

"What is your name?" I asked.

He glanced down as if both surprised and pleased by my question. "Porter."

"It is nice to meet you, Mr. Porter." I stopped and offered my hand. He was the first one to be friendly, and I knew how valuable that could be. I thought it was polite, but he was still walking and did not notice my gesture. I hurried to catch up. "Are you the butler? I didn't know people still had butlers."

"Something like that."

He glanced back at the closed dining room door, and I had trouble reading the brief expression I saw on his face.

It passed as quickly as it had come, and he returned his attention to the task of taking me to my room.

"My dad used to live here." I informed him, stopping to examine one of the pictures. "He was searching for a treasure hidden in the caverns below the estate."

"There are many legends in an old house like this one," Porter answered in his soft quiet voice.

"Do you know if they are true? Is there really a mine shaft that goes down into the caverns?" I had moved ahead and was walking backwards to watch his face. It was strangely stoic, giving nothing away.

"These stairs will take you to your room." Porter gestured to a doorway on the left that I had passed. "After you." He gave a little bow and waited.

Retracing my steps, I entered the stairway. "Am I to be up in the garret tower then?" I asked when we started up the second winding staircase.

Porter's smile appeared again. "No, Polly, you are to be in a spacious guest room with a good view of the grounds."

It was my turn to smile. This would be much better than the cots and corners where I had stayed in the past. I had never had a room all to myself and had to be careful not to let my imagination run ahead of reality. We went up two winding flights before he indicated I was to take the final doorway into the hall. The wooden floor was covered down the middle with a long thin carpet. When I paused to take it in, Porter passed me. He stopped at the first door on the left, and pushed it open. "If you need anything, Martha is in the room at the other end of the hall on the same side as yours. She handles housekeeping and can get you anything you need." Porter paused, looking at my backpack. "Is that the only bag you have?"

"Not exactly. I have a suitcase too." I tried not to let my irritation at my uncle spill over on to Porter. "My uncle forgot to unload it. He will probably find it in a few days and bring it back. Or send it with someone."

Porter's expression grew sad, but he did not say anything else about it. "I hope you rest very well, Polly," he said with a slight bow.

"I shall do my best," I responded, pulling out the edges of my jeans as I curtsied back.

He grinned, and his breath escaped as if he would laugh. He caught himself, checking the hall to ensure no one had witnessed his moment of weakness. "Listen, Polly, I like you. But being too friendly with the guests could cost me my job. I won't be able to talk to you much after this. It is how your Grandfather prefers to be served." He glanced past me to make sure the hall was still clear.

Following his example, I checked the hall before asking, "Could we be secret friends?"

He must have seen how much I wanted it because he hesitated, seeming to read the longing in my eyes. "You know, ones that don't even let on that they know each other," I added hopefully.

Porter looked relieved. "But who have each other's back in a pinch?" he finished softly.

"Yes, that kind of friends."

"We will be secret friends then." Porter gave a little bow and turned to go. The hall was dim, and I could have imagined it, but as he turned away, I thought I saw his cheerful face cloud with emotion.

I smiled bravely in case he turned to wave. When he disappeared into the stair entrance, I slipped into my room.

"A secret friend is better than no friend at all," I told myself. The door closed behind me as I leaned against it. My tears made it impossible to see my new room. Sinking down, I wrapped my arms around my legs. I rested my forehead on my knees, and let myself cry it out without a sound.

# Chapter 2

"Good morning, Grandfather." I walked down the long table to the chair that had been mine the night before. It was not until I was seated that I noticed the second man at the table. He sat to my Grandfather's left, his muscular arms resting on the table. The first thing I noticed about him was that his eyes were hard. When you get shuffled around as much as I have, you learn to see things about people that others miss.

I smiled at him politely, not sure if I was supposed to be seen and not heard at this point. Porter entered with a tray. On it was a bowl of fruit, a bowl I could not see into, and a platter of cooked meat that smelled like bacon from where I sat. After Porter had served Grandfather and his bulky, dark-haired guest, he came toward my end of the table. I looked up at him, and he smiled at me with only his eyes. I returned the secret smile. Funny how people can communicate with just their eyes. He dished some food from each bowl onto my plate, cocking his eyebrow slightly when I refused the oatmeal that was in the third bowl.

I looked down the table at Grandfather. He was deep in conversation with the stranger. Eating slowly, I listened hard to what they were saying without looking at them.

"The kid is small enough," the stranger protested glancing my way.

I bit off a piece of cantaloupe and made a show of prancing my fork around like the remaining cantaloupe was its hair. If they thought I was a distracted child, they would be freer with their talk.

Grandfather's low response was hard to understand.

"Look, no one wants the kid. That's why she is here," the man pointed out bluntly.

Grandfather shushed him, but I made no indication that I had heard. They were talking about the mine shaft down to the caverns. My father was convinced that there was a hidden treasure down there. He spent years talking about it. When I was five, I knew all about the legends of confederate soldiers hiding their stash in a mine and dying in battle before they could come back for it, and that drove my mom crazy. After my Mom and Dad split up, he came here to find the treasure. I'm not sure what happened, only that he stopped contacting us. Later, he died, and Mom said that I couldn't go to the funeral. The conversation at the other end of the table drew my attention again.

"Put her down. Have her search for it. If she doesn't come back to the shaft with the treasure, she doesn't come back up."

A murmuring response from Grandfather brought an outburst from the stranger. "No one cares, Henry. The kid is perfect. Put her down the mine. We have waited too long for this."

"You have a mine?" I asked, eagerly.

"It is not polite to listen to other people's conversations," Grandfather was glowering at the stranger, not me, as he spoke.

"Sorry, Grandfather." I decided to play the innocent child and see how far it got me.

"Grandfather?" the stranger looked amused.

"Be quiet, West. You have said too much already."

"Now that I know there's a mine," I ventured hesitantly, "Could you take me to see it sometime, Grandfather?"

"How would you like to go down in it?" West offered.

I wrinkled my nose, trying to look nervous so that they would think I was scared. "Is it dark, and are there spiders?" In reality, I didn't mind either.

West's face contorted into a hard, unpleasant grin. "No, it's a nice, clean mine shaft. You would get to ride down in a big bucket. Wouldn't that be fun?"

I decided they did not know the difference between a three-year-old and an 11 year old. "How do the miners get down? Do they use the bucket too?" I could tell right away that I had hit a sore spot.

"It is a closed mine. The bucket shaft was for supplies and is too narrow for a grown man to go down," Grandfather informed me. I wondered if he was catching onto my innocent act.

"Oh, then I would like to go down there." I popped a grape into my mouth to avoid saying more.

"See, Henry, your granddaughter would like to explore the nice, clean mine. It would give her something fun to do besides snooping around your big, old house."

By the way he said it, I figured there were some things in this old house that grandfather did not want to be discovered. "I don't mind exploring the house for a few days," I said with a smile. "But I would like to see the mine sometime. If you are ever going that way, maybe I could ride along."

The men exchanged looks, and I knew I was in.

# Chapter 3

"Polly, you can't go into the mine. It is not safe." Porter had stopped me at the top of the stairs. He was holding a screwdriver in one hand and a bit of wire in the other.

"What are you doing up here?" I asked. "Isn't this Martha's domain?"

"I'm repairing something for her. Polly, please," Porter stopped when my attention was drawn to something behind him.

My eyes darted to his, conveying a warning.

"Get some rest while you are here, too," Porter said as if that had been his original topic. "You will have plenty of time to explore the gardens. Your Grandfather mentioned your rumpled appearance at breakfast and would like you to take more care in the mornings. Maybe some extra sleep would help."

"What are you doing?" It was West.

"Good Morning, Mr. West." Porter gave the man one of his short, crisp bows. "I am repairing an old radio for Martha, Sir. I do hope I did not disturb you."

Eyeing the screwdriver and wire skeptically, West searched Porter's eyes for any sign that the servant was hiding something. Porter had been a silent aid for too long to make such a slip. He met West's eyes without flinching.

"Well, get on with your work. There's no reason for you to be hanging around the kid."

"It was my fault, Sir." I told him. "I came to breakfast looking rumpled, and he had a message of correction from my grandfather."

West looked amused. The same look he got anytime the title Grandfather was used in connection to the man he called Henry. "No harm was done. Go back to your play things." He left us, stopping to open and enter the third door from mine. At least I knew where he was for now.

"Thank you," I whispered.

Porter nodded silently. For all we knew, West could be listening at his door. Slipping past me, he disappeared down the staircase.

I went to my room and looked at myself in the mirror. I was anything but pretty. My straight brown hair was still in yesterday's hair tie which had slipped down in the night. I had fallen asleep when I had my cry by the door and had awakened stiff and cold at Martha's firm knock. Unzipping my backpack, I rummaged around until I found my travel sized hair brush. I pulled out the hair tie and started tackling my tangled locks. As I did, I thought back over what I had heard at breakfast. West wanted Grandfather, or Henry, to put me down the narrow shaft to find the treasure. I wondered if I would be given supplies. The shaft must have been for bringing up samples or putting down supplies. Somewhere in the caverns there would have been another entrance the miner's would have used. If someone had taken the time to close up the entrance, they must have been afraid people would still think the treasure was inside. Only, once it was closed, they had no way of looking for it. I paused and met my own green eyes in the mirror. Unless, they had been putting kids down the hole all this time. I thought of all the kids lost and starving as they wandered through the endless labyrinths of tunnels, trying desperately to find the treasure that would buy them their freedom.

I shivered and smiled. No use letting my imagination run away with me. I would see what I could find out today and go from there. I would need to start stashing food if I wanted to have it down in the tunnel. There was nothing from breakfast that could be saved. I split my hair into two sections and started braiding one. I would need a day or two to prepare. Anything I could use would need to fit into my backpack, if they would let me carry it. I smiled at myself in the mirror. I was not old enough to have forgotten how to throw a fit. I had not done it for at least six years, but I knew I could do it again if needed. They would let me keep the bag, or I wouldn't go down.

Tossing the finished braid over my shoulder, I felt the hair tie tap my shoulder bone. My hair was getting long again. That is how I liked it. I started in on the second braid, my thoughts going as fast as my fingers. I would need a flashlight and extra batteries. I had one, but it got put in my suitcase in the rush to get out the door. I let my mind ponder that for a few moments. Why was it so urgent that I left Uncle Matt's? Did it have something to do with the visitor he had the night before? They had stayed up very late talking together in hushed tones. Uncle Matt's wife, who said I could not call her Aunt Shelly, had told me not to be a snoop and to go to bed. She watched TV later than they talked, so there was no way I was going to overhear anything they said.

I tossed my second braid over my shoulder. With it, I also tossed out the memory of that night for now. There was no point in stewing over it when I didn't have enough information to figure anything out yet.

Shouldering my backpack, I headed down the hall toward Martha's room. I made sure to swing wide around the room West had entered, just in case.

I knocked on the door, but there was no answer. Going past her room into the shadowy end of the hall, I discovered a second staircase identical to the one I used to get to my room. Going down it, I found myself on the second floor. I peered down the dim hall. It was empty, and yet somehow very creepy to be there alone. I continued down the stairs to the ground floor. The smells that filled the hall made it easy to know what was where. To the right was the smell of food. To the left, I smelled laundry soap and cleaning supplies. Having no idea when I would be put down the hole, I decided food was more pressing than the flashlight. People can survive without light. I wondered briefly if living in the dark would make a person's eyes change so that they could see at night like a nocturnal animal. With a shrug I dismissed it. Dad had always said that God made us perfectly. I remembered the day I had run to find him at the neighbors where he was building them a new decorative brick wall for their patio. I had told him excitedly that my teacher at school had told me that monkeys turned into people. He picked me up, sat me on the stack of bricks, and looked me in the eyes.

"Polly, your teacher lied to you today," he had said. "Nothing turns into people, and people don't turn into anything else. God designed people perfectly to be people, and He said that His design was very good. Don't let anyone trick you into believing anything else."

I chewed my lip to keep back the sadness that the memory brought. I loved my dad.

"Are you alright, miss?"

I looked up to see a younger lady wearing a colorful apron staring at me over the biscuits she was cutting out on the island counter.

"Who are you talking to, Jane?" I heard another lady ask from somewhere beyond my line of sight.

"The little girl who came to the house last night," Jane answered. "She's here in the doorway looking as if she might cry."

An older, plump lady came around to where she could see me. She was drying her hands on a towel. "Well bless my soul, so she is. Are you lost?"

"No, Ma'am. I was looking around and followed the good smells in here."

"Ah, don't try your pretty flattery on me, young lady. It might work out there," she gestured with the towel she held toward the dining room. "I've had kids of my own. There will be no snitching scraps between meals in this house."

"But she's so skinny and sad looking, Miss Ella," Jane appealed. "Surely we have a little something she could take with her to explore the gardens."

Miss Ella shook her head, giving me a knowing smile. "Give her some of those old biscuits. You won't need them with all the fresh ones you are making."

With a happy smile, Jane hurried away, wiping her floured hands on her apron.

"Don't you make a habit of this, young lady," Miss Ella scolded with a twinkle in her eye. "If Mr. Blossom catches wind of this, we won't hear the end of it."

"Who is Mr. Blossom?" I asked, looking with interest around the large kitchen.

The cooks looked at each other in amazement.

"He owns this whole place, Dear."

"I think you call him Grandfather." Jane glanced at Miss Ella, and I did not miss the odd look that passed between them.

I took the biscuits Jane gave me. She had put three into a zip-topped bag. I was grateful, knowing that would keep them fresh.

"The fastest way to the gardens is out this back hall. There's a door on your right just before the laundry," Jane told me. "I sometimes slip out there for a breath of fresh air when I get a minute between meals."

Thanking them both, I left the kitchen and headed for the laundry room. Three biscuits was not much of a stash for surviving underground caverns, but it was a start. I stopped in the hall to slip them inside my backpack between the folds of my hoodie. I hoped that would keep them from being crushed, but I could survive on crumbs just as well as on biscuits.

Shrugging my backpack into place, I headed down the hall once more. Passing the outside door Jane had described, I continued on down the hall. I could hear someone moving around in the laundry room. I stopped at the doorway and saw a middle-aged woman with wildly frizzy hair. The blonde-brown frizz was pulled back into a loose hair tie at the base of her neck in a haphazard way.

"Excuse me," I called over the noise of the four washing machines that whirred industriously.

She looked around, startled. Seeing me, she smiled and came to greet me.

"Polly, isn't it?" she asked cheerfully.

"Yes, Ma'am. Are you Miss Martha?"

"Just Martha is fine. Miss Ella likes the extra fuss, but I'm not one to take on titles I don't need to carry." She pulled a load of towels out of one of the dryers and carried it to the folding table just inside the laundry room door. "But you didn't ask for my life story, did you?"

"Porter said I should come to you if I need anything."

"What is it you need, Sweetie?" Martha asked pulling out a towel and folding it quickly.

"Could I have a flashlight?"

Pausing on her second fold, Martha looked me over. "Why would you need a flashlight?" she asked. I saw she was doing some thinking behind her cheery smile.

"I had one before I came," I explained truthfully. "But it got put in my suitcase and that didn't make it out of my uncle's car. I'm not scared of the dark," I added quickly. "I just like to have one, in case."

Several more towels had joined Martha's growing stack. She glanced at me, and her eyes were glossy as if she might cry. "It is hard being moved around, isn't it Polly?"

I didn't want to cry but her empathy touched something deep inside me. I bit my bottom lip and blinked hard.

Martha's arms came around me, and she held me tight. It felt good to have someone care. A little sob escaped me, but I managed to keep back my tears.

Releasing me, Martha looked me in the eyes as if seeing into my soul. "What else do you need, Polly?"

"I don't have any pajamas," I blurted out. I had not planned to tell her, but Martha really did care.

"What about a toothbrush?" she asked retrieving a little note pad from the far corner of the room where a messy desk collected everything that did not belong in the laundry. She made a few notes and looked at me expectantly.

"I have a toothbrush, and a hair brush too." The little things mean more when they are all you own.

Martha was thorough, and in a few minutes she had several more items written down on her paper.

"I will send Porter into town to get what he can today." Martha promised.

"And a flashlight?" I reminded her.

She nodded, jotting it down on her list.

"And..." I hesitated, not wanting to press my luck.

"And?" Martha asked.

"Well, would extra batteries be too much? It's not that I'm afraid of the dark," I added. I was needy, but I was not a liar. I had no intention of tricking Martha into helping me.

"Not at all." Martha said slowly as she added them to the list.

I looked around the crowded room. When I turned back

to her, Martha was watching me.

I frowned a little, wondering what she was thinking.

"If you need anything at all, come and tell me," Martha said at length.

Smiling, I nodded. "Thank you, Martha."

# Chapter 4

The gardens were expansive and impressive. I thought Grandfather must be very rich to own a garden that was bigger than any park I had ever seen. Everything was neatly trimmed, and I don't think I saw one weed in the perfectly trimmed hedges and distinct flowerbeds. Benches had been placed thoughtfully along the winding paths, giving visitors many opportunities to relax and enjoy the fragrant blossoms. The huge garden was hemmed in by majestic mountains on three sides.

In the center of the garden was a large fountain that spilled over three steps of decorative brickwork into the little moat that surrounded it. The backside of the fountain, the side furthest from the big house, was made of a flat and uninteresting wall of brick with a metal panel in the middle. It had a key hole in it and no handle. I guessed that the fountain controls were inside. Going around to the front, I watched the water swell and pour down over the steps into the rocky trench that surrounded it. This too was encased in a low decorative brick wall. Climbing onto the little wall, I peered into the pool and saw there was a pipe in it where the fountain could be switched to spray up before it flowed down over the brick steps. Wandering over to one of the benches opposite the front of the fountain, I sat watching the water for a long time. Something about it was pulling at a memory I could not seem to grasp.

Frustrated, I gave up and headed out of the garden in the direction of the road. There, as I had hoped, was a sign telling of the nearby sites. The third site listed was the Weatherbee Mine. The arrow pointed up and to the left toward one of the nearby mountains. A winding trail started from the sign and disappeared into the boulders strewn across the mountain. By the strip of grass down the middle, I assumed the trail was used more by four wheelers than tourists out for a stroll.

I looked around, Dad had always said that the caverns were under the main mansion and that the original entrance had been forgotten or destroyed. This path led away from the house. Unless I was mistaken, the caverns that my dad came to explore were not that far from the house.

I looked around for any sign of the mine shaft. I could see why everyone talked about the gardens. The landscape around the mansion was rocky and covered in a thin dry grass. Yet somehow the green, flowering garden thrived in the middle of this desert-like land.

"Looking for something?"

West's voice made me jump, and I turned quickly to face him. "You scared me!" I told him, buying myself time.

"Sorry about that. Are you ready to go see the mine?"

"I wouldn't have to go down today, right?" I asked, sub-consciously stepping away from him.

"No, not today. You can look at it first."

I did not believe the oily way he said it. "I am a little nervous and would like Grandfather to be here when I go down. No offense."

"A look wouldn't hurt."

I remembered the pictures in my childhood Bible of the snake talking to Eve in the garden. West would have made a good snake. "I know, but I, well, I think tomorrow would be better."

He was not convinced. For an instant, I thought he would

grab my arm and march me to the mine.

Martha came out on the porch and vigorously shook a rug out over the front steps. The wind caught the dust, carrying it toward us in a little cloud.

Seeing her, West seemed to change his mind. He shrugged, "That's a good idea. That way we can get an early start tomorrow."

I nodded, swallowing the cold fear that had welled up inside. "Good plan," I said lamely.

I don't remember if I said good-bye or not, but I got back to the house as quickly as I could.

———

The next morning at breakfast, Porter cleared his throat all through the meal and left the room often to fetch little things for the meal that no one needed. His irregular behavior set us all on edge. Normal conversation was almost impossible, even between West and Grandfather, as Porter's throat clearing seemed to indicate he wanted to say something or keep someone else from speaking.

Finally, when I had finished my scrambled eggs and was working on my jelly spread toast, Grandfather exploded.

"For heaven's sake, man. Either speak up or stop that infernal noise you are making. If you can't stand quietly, perhaps you should call in the cook's assistant to take your place."

Porter looked shocked. "I'm very sorry, Sir. I did not realize I was disturbing your meal."

"Disturbing my meal? You have ruined my appetite completely," Grandfather fumed. "What is the meaning of this? Speak up, your job is on the line."

I saw Porter's normally stoic face change for an instant. Once again, I saw the fleeting expression I had seen on the first night. Despite Grandfather's threat, it was not fear I had seen in his eyes. For some reason, Porter seemed to have no fear of losing his position. Beneath his humble servant's behavior, was he silently challenging Grandfather's authority over him?

Grandfather had seen Porter's expression change, and it made him flustered and angry. "Speak up, man," Grandfather commanded.

"I seem to have caught a cold last night, Mr. Blossom," Porter looked directly at West who was watching with a strange, slightly amused expression.

Grandfather did not miss the accusing look.

"I don't think the cough will last long." Standing straight backed before his employer, Porter waited without expression.

Grandfather took his napkin from his lap and laid in on the table. "I will discuss this further with you in my study."

"Yes, Sir." Porter did not look my way as he came forward to clear Grandfather's place. When he slipped through the door to the kitchen, we heard the dishes clatter as if set down in a hurry. A moment later, we all heard him coughing in the hall as he distanced himself from the dining room.

"He is pretty sick," I observed. "Will you fire him for getting sick, Grandfather?"

"I am not his nursemaid, child. His health is his responsibility."

I slid my half eaten toast to the middle of my plate and laid my napkin on the table as Grandfather had done. I wasn't hungry anymore. "There was a cold wind last night. I could feel it from my bed."

"I will have the housekeeper check your window, drafts will raise the utility bill and drive the guests away." Grandfather rose. "For the time being, no one is to go to the mine shaft," he announced firmly looking first at West and then at me. "There is a heaviness in the air, and rain would make the shaft and caverns very dangerous. Do you understand?" Again he looked at West before looking down the table at me.

We both nodded. West looked irritated and rose as Porter entered from the kitchen door. Porter came to my end of the table and silently collected my plate and silverware.

"Thank you." I was rewarded by a tired smile as he retreated from the table.

West stalked from the room, and we heard the front door shut hard.

Porter returned once more to clear West's place.

"You looked at West as if your being sick was his fault." Grandfather had apparently decided to have it out here instead of waiting until they were in his office.

Porter stopped his work and gave Grandfather his attention.

I slid slowly down in my seat, hoping not to draw attention to myself. There were dishes to be collected, but Porter stood facing Grandfather without so much as a glance at the table.

"What happened last night?" Grandfather asked.

Porter cleared his throat, "I went to my room last night after the doors were checked and could see at once that my room had been searched."

Grandfather's thick eyebrows shot up in surprise. I slid lower, my elbows were now resting on the chair cushion and I could just see over the top of the table.

Grandfather gave an irritated grunt. "Why didn't you come to me?"

"It was late, Sir. I did not wish to bother you." Porter shifted his weight slightly. "If I may say so, Mr. Blossom, you are not quite yourself since Mr. West and the child arrived."

Grandfather's brows dropped low and his voice was like a growl. "That is none of your business, Porter."

"Very well, but be careful, Sir."

For a moment, they faced each other silently.

Retrieving his napkin from the table, Grandfather casually wiped his mouth and leaned back in his chair. "What else happened?"

Porter cleared his throat. "Naturally, I was concerned that something was stolen." Porter cleared his throat several times, and his eyes started to water.

Grandfather looked annoyed. "Go cough in the hall."

Porter hurried out, his deep coughing rang through the empty hall. There was a delay, and when he reentered the room, he slipped a cough drop into his mouth.

"What do you remember after you entered your room?" Grandfather prompted.

So far neither of them had even glanced in my direction. I knew I should slip down out of sight, but I didn't want to miss what was going on.

Porter hesitated, but seemed to change his mind about whatever he wanted to say. "I thought the vandal had gone, so I crossed my room to check my belongings without looking around first. Something hard struck me, and I woke this morning to find myself sprawled on the floor, chilled to the bone. That is all I know."

"And with no real evidence you are putting the blame on West?" Grandfather demanded. I wondered if he was actually angrier with West than he was with Porter. I was in the process of slipping under the table, my knees were on the floor but my head and shoulders remained on my seat. I froze, waiting. From my awkward position I could no longer see their faces.

"The doors were locked, Sir, and Mr. West is the only guest staying in the main house." Porter pointed out.

"That is your evidence?" Grandfather bellowed. "There are plenty of staff in the house overnight. And the child."

For the first time they realized I was not in my seat. I slipped the rest of the way under the thick wood of the table, waiting breathlessly for them to go on.

"Where is the child?" Grandfather demanded.

Porter, occupied with his defense had not noticed me sinking down as they talked. The tablecloth hid me from their view. From my vantage point, I saw Porter's polished shoes move toward my end of the table.

"I don't know, Sir. Perhaps she went up to her room. I can check if you like," Porter offered.

"I don't care where she is." I could hear the frustration in Grandfather's voice. "You are changing the subject. What else happened last night? I demand that you tell me."

Porter's feet turned back toward my Grandfather's seat. "I do not wish to point a finger with so little proof, but I trust the staff, and the child does not have the strength to strike me with such force."

"Jane, come in here," Grandfather bellowed.

Jane appeared a minute later. I peered out without moving the cloth and could tell by the way she was tugging and smoothing that she had thrown on a clean apron to appear before my Grandfather. I could not see her face which meant that she could not see mine, but I scooted to the middle to be safe.

"You called, Sir?" Jane gave a little curtsy.

"Feel his head."

I smiled to myself, imagining the awkward looks that accompanied the silence that followed.

"Porter's head, Sir?" Jane asked timidly.

I heard Grandfather's breath come in a strong irritated blast. "Do you see anyone else?"

"No, Sir." Jane's feet shifted.

"You don't believe me." Porter's statement was tense. "Why would I make up such a damaging story?"

Grandfather's answer was smooth, "You have made it clear by your behavior that you do not enjoy West's visits to the Weatherbee Retreat."

Porter did not protest.

"I am simply verifying your story. Jane?"

I saw Jane's feet move toward Porter, his pant legs moved as if he were bending toward her.

"Mercy me, Mr. Blossom! He's got a goose egg the size of my fist on his head!" Jane exclaimed. "How did it happen?"

"That is all, Jane." Grandfather dismissed her, and she curtsied once more before leaving the room.

For several seconds no one spoke.

"How on earth can you prove that someone looked through your belongings?" Grandfather's sudden outburst startled me.

"There was clothing hanging out of my drawers and loose papers on my dresser, Sir." Porter rolled the cough drop around in his mouth rapidly to diffuse the cough that was pushing its way up his throat. I could hear it clicking against his teeth. "You know where I stand in regards to West, but I believe I have been employed long enough for you to know that I would not make such accusations without cause. I would not have told you if you had not asked me directly."

"Very well, I will consider the information you have given me." Grandfather rose, signaling the end of the conversation.

I watched beneath the tablecloth as Grandfather's long stride took him from the room.

A few seconds passed, and then I heard Porter coughing above me. Once he had recovered, he began collecting the glasses and miscellaneous items on the table. I could hear the soft clatter through the table top as he stacked them onto West's empty plate.

I waited until Porter had left the room before slipping from my hiding place and out the dining room door.

As I climbed the stairs, I wondered what West could have been looking for in Porter's room. Did Porter know something about the treasure? Could he have been working for Grandfather when my dad was living on the estate?

I thought of the fountain. Something about that structure stuck in my mind. What connection could it have with the treasure and my dad's death?

# Chapter 5

"Grandfather?"

He clapped the book he was reading shut and hid it in his lap behind his large mahogany desk. "What are you doing in here?" he demanded. "You are never to come into my study without permission."

I blinked at him in surprise.

"What do you want?"

"Was that book my dad's?" It was not what I had intended to ask, but the sight of the worn journal had triggered memories I thought were forgotten. I had lived with both my mom and my dad until I was almost 9. A few months before they split up, my dad had gotten the thick leather bound journal from a friend. He had told me he would use it to record important things and special events he did not want to forget. Though I was not allowed to open it, I had admired the worn leather cover many times and would recognize its distinct markings anywhere.

"It is mine," Grandfather corrected with a strange gleam in his eyes.

"But it was his. I recognize it." I knew I should let it go, but I could not. Dad would have written in it before he died. Mom would not tell me how he had died, and I needed to know.

"There are many journals that look the same in this world, child."

"My name is Polly." I blurted. "I'm not a child. I'm eleven years old. My dad died here, and I have a right to know how it happened."

Grandfather looked amused. "Even if it was his journal, he would not have written about his death in it. Your father got sick and died. There was nothing mysterious about it."

I stood staring at him, wondering at the cold way he could talk about my dad's death.

"Is there anything else?" His voice seemed to drip with fake politeness.

"Do you ever turn the fountain off?"

"The fountain?" He seemed taken back by the question. "No, why would we."

"Even in the winter?" I pressed.

His brows came down over his eyes. "Why do you want to know?"

"I have never seen a fountain like it," I answered honestly. "That is what I came to ask you before I got distracted by the journal."

He relaxed visibly. "Yes, sometimes in the winter we do drain the fountain. I'm sorry to disappoint you but this may be one of the last cold weeks this winter. And it is not cold enough to harm the fountain. The spring flowers are already up. The fountain will remain on until late in the fall."

I nodded. "Grandfather?"

He looked at me as if he did not trust me.

"Will you come with me when I go to see the mine and am put down into the shaft?"

Again, I had managed to catch him off guard, and he did not enjoy the feeling. "Can't you stay on one subject?" he smoothed the long white mustache that draped down the sides of his mouth.

"West scares me. I am afraid he would leave me down there." I saw his eyes drop to the journal on his lap.

When he looked up at me again, it was with a cold, hard look that scared me. "Yes, Polly, I will go with you." He paused, as if he had thought of something pleasant. He added, "And we can bring Porter too if that makes you feel better."

"I think if you are there that will be enough." I did not want to get Porter into trouble. "Mom trusted you enough to send me here, so I think she would feel better about me going with you."

Grandfather's laugh was sarcastic. "She didn't send you here because she trusted me. She sent you because she needed to get you off her hands."

"That's not true." I blurted even though I knew it was. Feeling the blood rushing to my face, I turned away. Knowing it would rile him, I wandered around his office, touching his books and trinkets here and there as a quiet way to get even.

He did not react.

"The weather should be clear in a day or so." Grandfather's voice was pleasant once more. "We will make it a grand excursion." His look gave me the same creepy feeling I'd gotten from staring into the eyes of a tiger at the zoo.

"Thank you." I backed out of the study door, pulling the door closed behind me. I would need to gather more supplies.

———

"Polly? Are you okay?"

I looked up to see Martha coming towards me over the short garden lawn.

Scrambling to my feet, I brushed the dirt from the front of my jeans. "Yes, I'm okay, I was just looking."

"Looking at what?" Martha still looked concerned.

"The fountain," I told her cheerfully. "I have never seen one like it before."

"Mr. Blossom had it custom built. I suppose it is interesting to watch the water flow over the steps." She smiled at me. "I've never stopped rushing around to really look at it before."

"Do you know who built it?" I asked.

Martha looked thoughtful. I know we had a bricklayer on site a few years ago. I heard that he did the fountain, the front steps to the main porch, and…" She looked thoughtful then laughed. "Anything brick around here was probably done by him. I came to work here only a few weeks before he finished up his projects and…moved on. He seemed nice, but most of his work was outside, so I did not know him well. I was busy in the house learning the new job. Porter would know though. He's been here four years, almost five now. Time flies when you are kept busy!" She looked worried and glanced at the house. "I need to get back. I'm working on getting the rooms cleaned and ready for when the guests start coming next month. I saw you go out earlier and wanted to check to make sure nothing happened to you." She paused and looked into my eyes. "Are you sure you are okay? It can be pretty lonely out here."

"I'm okay. I was just bored so I thought I would watch the water a while."

"It isn't much fun, but you could come help me with the rooms if you want," Martha offered.

"I would love to!" I exclaimed eagerly. Anything would beat trying to avoid Mr. West and Grandfather in the big empty house they called the retreat.

"If you are sure you want to, I would love the company." Martha put her arm around my shoulders, and we started back toward the house together.

———

Nights were long and lonely in the big house. I could see

now the benefits of being pushed into a little house where there was no room for you. When I had stayed with my aunts and uncles, I had wished for a little personal space. Now, the whole house echoed with personal space. If I wanted, I could go most of the day without seeing anyone at all except at meals.

Opening my notebook, I laid it on the bed and flopped down next to it. Page one had a list of supplies I wanted for the trip down the mine. I ran my finger down the list. Most of the important things were marked off. The only problem was that the trip kept getting postponed. I was not sure my food supplies would be any good whenever the day finally came. Grandfather's excuse was always that it looked like rain. Not knowing when I would actually be put down the shaft set me on edge. After several sunny days I wondered if they were waiting for my uncle to remember my bag and bring it by. After that happened, no one would care what happened to me for months or even years.

I mentally set that aside. Reaching under the far pillow of my queen sized bed, I pulled out a book about mines. I had discovered it hidden away in a cluttered storage room. It had a section about the Forgotten Mine, so I had brought it up to my room to study at night. The book contained a rough map that I had copied into my notebook, some estimated elevation figures, and a few other titbits about the possibility of a treasure stash dating back to the civil war. The most helpful part was the new section I had just gotten to. There were a few of those old pictures where everything is grey that showed mine tunnels and land experts who wore funny old fashioned clothes. Those were interesting, but tucked into the book were several more recent pictures. One was a color shot of the Forgotten Mine shaft mostly hidden by tall grass, and a few slightly blurry shots that looked like they were taken inside the caverns beneath the ground. In one of them, there was a white smudge on the wall near the edge of the picture. It was hard to tell if the smudge was part of the picture or if the photo had been damaged when it was developed.

Laying the three pictures out on the bed, I examined them closely. It was exciting to know I was looking inside the Forgotten Mine, but I could not find anything helpful in either of the blurry shots. I picked up the book to read more. As I moved it, the corner of the book caught on a picture, flipping it over on the comforter. There on the back, in my dad's clear handwriting were the words, "photo by Mason Hamilton."

I snatched up the picture and examined it again. My dad had been inside the Forgotten Mine!

# Chapter 6

"Hi Polly, are you enjoying yourself today?" Martha and Porter were wrestling a large rolled rug out onto the wide porch.

"Yes, it's such a pretty day." I had been out skipping rope all through the trails of the garden. I was hot and happy. The light breeze was cool on my bare arms. I climbed the porch steps to watch them drape the rug over the porch rail. It started to slip, and they both grabbed at their edge to keep it from crushing the phlox that bloomed in the flowerbed below.

Martha pushed a bit of her voluminous hair from her face, leaving a streak of dust. There was evidence on her face that it wasn't the first time she had done that. "That was close!" she gasped.

Porter, still holding his side from falling, was coughing into his elbow. He was wearing a short sleeved polo and jeans.

He recovered himself and caught me looking at him. "What are you grinning at?" he asked good-naturedly.

"You look different in those normal clothes. I'm so used to seeing you all dressed up in your button up shirts and stuff. You look nice all covered in dust."

He laughed, which sent him into another short coughing fit. "If you weren't a guest, I'd show you how nice you could look," he threatened with a grin.

I climbed up on the section of porch rail behind Martha.

"Don't hide behind me," she laughed, going to retrieve

an old fashioned rug paddle from where it was propped by the front door.

"Why don't you just vacuum the rug?" I asked, winding up my jump rope. I had discovered it earlier that day and had enjoyed the much needed entertainment.

Martha looked over at Porter who looked amused. "Why don't you tell her? You serve closer to the master."

"Be careful," he cautioned seriously, and Martha looked around to see if Grandfather was around. She thanked him with her eyes and set to work on the rug.

"It's like this, Polly," Porter came to stand up by me where the dust would not reach him. "Mr. Blossom is very particular about how his house is kept clean. The rugs are vacuumed through the week, but twice a year, they must be taken out and beaten."

"I guess that makes sense." I could see by the billowing clouds of dust that Martha's labors were effective. "But I would just buy a stronger vacuum."

Porter laughed and coughed. "You will get to pick when you have your own place."

I got quiet. I wondered if I would ever have a house of my own. My mom never had. Not since she left dad. I stretched out my leg on the wide top board of the porch rail, enjoying the warm sun. "Porter?"

"Yes, Ma'am?"

I smiled at his formality. "Did you know my dad?"

His face was suddenly unreadable. He had put on the slightly pleasant mask he wore while waiting on us at the dinner table.

"You did, didn't you?" I pressed eagerly. "Martha said you were here when the brick layer was employed, and my dad was a mason by trade."

"Martha sometimes talks more than she should," Porter answered, going to help her turn the rug.

"But he was here, and I think he built the fountain and the steps and…"

"It's a beautiful day, you should go and enjoy it," he pointed out.

I fell silent. That was the most polite way I had ever been asked to go away.

I watched as they wrestled the rug into place, and Porter took a turn with the paddle. The dirt flew in a cloud that the wind swept away down the long driveway.

"What did you say to him?" Martha asked leaning against the rail. "He looks like he's going to break through the rail with that paddle."

"I asked him about my dad." I sighed. "I didn't know it would make him upset."

Martha watched him for a minute. "Porter probably needs to let off some steam. He has a hard position, Polly. Mr. Blossom expects him to stand within hearing range without ever hearing anything or expressing any type of emotion. All that pent up feeling has to go somewhere. I don't think he's mad at you."

"I think the bricklayer was Mason Hamilton." I saw recognition in her face.

"How would you know that?" She eyed me skeptically.

"He was my dad."

She sputtered a little, looked away, and self-consciously adjusted her hair tie that never seemed to slip from its place. "Polly," she finally said. "When I talked about the brick layer, well, I didn't know he was your father." She looked over at Porter, her eyes sad. "It was hard on Porter when your dad left."

Porter paused to look over at her.

Clearing her throat, Martha changed the subject. "The slower times between tourist seasons are hard on us all. In a few weeks, more staff will be coming on to help us handle all the work when the guests arrive. We are starting late this year. Something about the weather. But it will get livelier here soon. You will enjoy all of the excitement. You might even find a friend your age to play with. Lots of people bring their kids."

I was only half listening to Martha. It puzzled me that Porter didn't want to talk about my dad.

Porter started coughing and went down to the far end of the long porch.

"Is that your last rug?" Miss Ella asked from the doorway. She was still wearing her dirty apron.

"Yes it is!" Martha looked relieved.

"Good. You get that rug back in and come around to the back porch. I just finished the kitchen floors and am in the mood to celebrate. Jane is pouring us all something cool to drink." Miss Ella looked at me and smiled, "Do you want to join us, Miss Polly?"

Despite Miss Ella's good natured warnings about spoiling me, I had found the kitchen an inviting place to be. There were times when they had even allowed me to help with some of the meal prep. Each time I had to agree not to tell Grandfather unless he asked me directly.

"Yes, Ma'am!" I slid off the rail and collected the rug paddle from where Porter had left it. He was coming back toward us, dusting himself off as he went.

"There's no use dusting yourself when you are about to wrestle this thing back inside," Martha informed him playfully.

He smiled back, but the laughter was gone from his eyes. When he heard about the cool drinks, he wavered as if afraid I would ask him more, and more afraid he wouldn't be there to keep the others from talking.

We wiped our feet well on the small porch rug and then they wrestled the big rug back through the front door which I held open for them. Once it was in its place in the expansive entryway, Porter declined Miss Ella's invitation, saying he would clean up and rest before dinner. He looked very tired. Even I knew a cough like that makes sleeping almost impossible at night.

The four of us ladies gathered on the back porch. It was smaller, almost like a deck, and brick steps led from it down to the lawn. Through the cracks between the wood I could see that there was a space underneath. That space could be helpful if I needed to evade West in the future. On the deck were three plastic chairs. It was a lot more casual than the fancy wooden benches and rockers on the front porch.

I sat on the top step to leave the chairs for the other ladies. That way I could see their faces. They talked about their chores and the tourists coming as we sipped our cold lemonade. The conversation slowed, and I waited. When no one spoke, I did. "Did any of you know Mason Hamilton? I think he was the mason Grandfather hired to do the bricks on the stairs and fountain."

"Convenient name for his line of work," Jane observed with a smile. When no one else laughed, she added seriously, "No, the fountain was here before I was hired."

"A little," Martha confessed. She seemed uncomfortable admitting it now that she knew he was my dad.

"What makes you ask?" Miss Ella's face gave her away.

"I really like the design of the fountain and wanted to know more about him." What I said was true, but not the whole story.

Martha cocked an eyebrow at me but said nothing.

"The fountain is an original design," Miss Ella said matter-of-factly. "Mason drew up the plans and Mr. Blossom let him build it. That fountain itself has attracted a lot of tourists because of its unique design. These steps were also built by him. All the wooden ones were giving out. Mason did the work in exchange for his room and board during the off season."

"Did he work all day on them?"

"Are you asking if he explored the mine, Polly?" Miss Ella was serious. "You know I don't like people trying to pry information out of me by asking round about questions."

"I know he explored it. That was why he was here. But how did he get into it?"

Miss Ella looked thoughtful. She was pretty in a motherly way. Her once brown hair that swooped gently up into her loose bun was fading to gray. It framed her face giving it a gentle softness.

I sipped my drink to give her time to remember.

"I suppose he went down the shaft," she finally answered. "He was as skinny as a rail for being someone who moved bricks all day."

I smiled, remembering that about Dad. He was strong, but as "lean as a doe in the winter" as he often said. "Why don't they make the shaft wider?"

Jane leaned forward, eager to share the tidbit she knew. "They say it's a nature made air shaft. If they use dynamite to expand it, the whole cavern might collapse, burying all of the history hidden inside. The shaft is the only known entrance. And," Jane paused dramatically. "There are legends of treasure hidden in the mine!"

"Look who's been listening to the tourist's gossip." Martha grinned, pushing her stray hair back from her face again.

"Besides," Jane added with an injured air, "Mr. Blossom doesn't want it widened. He doesn't want people poking around there looking for the treasure. There's some young guys who like to mess around near the shaft. Mr. Blossom sends to Porter run them off now and then."

Martha pretended to be impressed. Jane ignored her.

"What happened to Mason after he finished the brick projects?" I picked a gnat out of my drink and flicked it into the bushes. I did not miss the looks exchanged by the ladies.

"I suppose we should get back in and finish up our spring cleaning," Miss Ella told us. She tipped her cup to drink the dregs of her lemonade. The ice clinked happily back down in her cup when she set it on the little table beside her.

I stood and faced them. "I'm not asking in a round-about way," I told the plump cook seriously. "Mason Hamilton was my dad, and I want to know what happened to him."

Miss Ella's eyes grew wide.

"What's all this?" West appeared around the corner of the house, coming along the neatly trimmed hedge to where we sat. "Is this what Mr. Blossom pays you for?"

"That's his business, not yours." Miss Ella was so sharp and firm with him that the rest of us could only stare.

West was flustered by her unexpected boldness. "Henry will hear about this," he threatened darkly.

"You can go tattle like a school child, but you will just look silly." Miss Ella retorted, making no move to rise from her seat. She looked down on him from the porch. "You are up to no good here, and we want no part of your schemes."

West glared at her, but it had no effect, and he had to give it up. He stalked away angrily.

"Now that he's gone, we will get back to the spring cleaning," Miss Ella announced. She rose and went into the house without another word, leaving us staring after her in amazement.

# Chapter 7

"Polly? Oh there you are! You are late for lunch, and Mr. Blossom sent me to find you." Martha's thick hair had come out of her loose pony tail in her mad rush to find me.

I jumped up, shoving my notebook and the other items under my pillow. "Coming!"

"You will never guess what happened just a few minutes ago." Martha and I were hurrying down the stairs side by side. "Your uncle dropped off your suitcase!"

"He brought it back?" I had begun to doubt that he would.

Nodding, Martha went on, "I told him to wait and I would fetch you, but he was as cool as a stranger. He walked up, set it on the porch, and drove off without so much as a hello."

"I'll run it up to your room while you are at lunch." Martha promised. She stopped me at the bottom of the stairs and looked me over.

"You don't look very happy about it."

"I am," I gave her a cheery smile. I truly was glad to have my things back, but I also knew this meant I would be going into the mine soon.

"If you say so." She brushed something off of my shoulder, apparently considering how to go on. "Polly, Mr. Blossom is not in a good mood this afternoon," she informed me softly. "So keep quiet at the table if you can."

Smiling bravely, I nodded.

She gave me a little push toward the dining room. "Better

run for it, or we will both be in trouble."

I ran, whispering, "Thank you, Martha!" over my shoulder.

Stopping at the door to smooth my hair and dress, I slipped into the dining room. Before Grandfather could scold, I said, "I am very sorry I am late. I did not keep track of the time which was inconsiderate."

There was nothing else to say, so Grandfather only grunted in response.

Porter brought the meal, and Grandfather and West spoke in low tones at the far end of the table. I could not hear enough to make any sense of what was said. I ate my food in silence, careful not to clink my silverware against my plate.

"Polly, the spring guests will arrive in a few weeks. We will go to the mine tomorrow morning early. Be at breakfast by 6 o'clock sharp."

I blinked at him, trying to grasp the sudden announcement after a long quiet meal. "Okay." I finally managed. "What should I wear?"

"You are going down a mine shaft. Why does it matter what you wear?" West grumbled. He had been grumping around the house and grounds since his run in with Miss Ella a few days ago. It had taken some quick maneuvering, but I had managed to avoid him outside of meal times.

"Sorry," I mumbled. Now that the day was almost here. I felt a sense of panic slowly rising inside. They had been so eager to put me down the first night. I had played along, wanting to go into the mine that my dad had been so passionate about. Now a week had passed, and I found myself dreading it. What Grandfather had said in his study came to mind. Had my mom really sent me there to get rid of me? What if they really were going to leave me down there? What if my mom had been in on the whole plot all along? I was in the way and made her uncomfortable. She didn't know about God like my dad. Dad said Jesus saved him and changed him when I was five. I don't really remember much about it when it happened. Only that he and mom didn't yell anymore. Well, she still yelled at him, but Dad didn't yell back. He was always doing little kind things for her and me, too. I missed him.

Suddenly the missing became too much to bear. I knew I was going to cry right there if I didn't get out quick.

"Excuse me," I mumbled and ran from the room. I stumbled up the stairs, fighting the tears that blurred my vision. Why had mom left him? Why did we have to move from place to place, staying until the landlords kicked us out for not paying? Why did she have to have guys over who didn't love her and made me feel dirty to be near them? I hit my shin and sat down to clutch my leg, rocking to sooth the pain. Why couldn't my mom have died instead of Dad?

As soon as I thought it, I knew it was wrong. My self-pity turned to anger. If they were going to put me down the mine to die, maybe it was better that way. No one actually cared what happened to me. Not really. Laying my head against the wall, I frowned, thinking angrily about all of the people who had let me down. A memory tugged at my mind, and I could almost hear my dad saying, "Polly, no matter what happens, God will always love you more than any human ever can. You are in His hands. Talk to Him and trust Him. He will take care of you."

My anger faded. Taking a deep breath, I stood up. I knew what I had to do.

————

The house was dark and still, it had been for almost half an hour. Watching the time pass on the old fashioned alarm clock that sat on the night stand by my bed had almost put me to sleep. I slipped from under my covers. It felt good to be in my own pajamas instead of Jane's long nightdress that I was always tripping over. Creeping to the door, I listened. Hearing a latch click softly in the direction of West's room, I froze.

A flashlight beam played across the bottom of my door before moving away. By laying on the floor I could see the light and the accompanying shadowy feet disappear into the stairwell.

I pulled open the door, and it didn't make a sound. I smiled. I had found a little bottle of oil in the garden shed after lunch and used it to silence the hinges, so I would be ready for tonight's mission. Only I had not planned on doing it with someone else wandering around, and had no desire to encounter West in the darkness.

Moving silently in my socked feet, I crept down the stone steps. Far enough behind to see the faint glow of his light up ahead.

A muffled exclamation below stopped me mid step. Holding my breath, I waited.

"I told you not to creep around this house at night." Grandfather's loud whisper carried well in the silence.

"I was coming to find you, Henry," West answered. "I have discovered a large hole in your plan of which you are apparently completely unaware. You delayed the trip too long. You should have put her down the morning after she arrived like I advised."

"What are you talking about?" Grandfather demanded, his voice rising slightly.

"Your dear little staff team has grown rather fond of your granddaughter, haven't they?"

By the silence, I could tell that West was right. Grandfather had not considered this before.

"If you go trooping off with her in the morning and don't come back with her, there will be a lot of questions asked, and the authorities will get involved," West murmured.

"Blast it all!" Grandfather was pacing down below, I could hear his muffled footsteps. "I suppose you have thought through a solution?"

"Yes, we will cancel the trip tomorrow and make sure everyone knows it. What can we do if she gets upset and runs away?" West's tone was ominous. I sped back up the steps. I would have to use the other stairs. My time was running out very quickly.

# Chapter 8

I jerked awake, glancing around in the dark for what had made the sound that woke me. I heard nothing besides the normal creaking of the big old house. Looking up at the old-fashioned clock, I saw the long hand was on the six. It must have been the soft night chime of the clock letting the house know it was twelve-thirty that had woken me. Shivering and scolding myself for falling asleep, I crept from the kitchen into the dining room. Crossing the room quietly, I peered through the double doors that led into the entryway. It was dark. Counting to ten slowly in my head, I waited. There was no movement or change that I could see through the crack. Pushing open one of the doors, I darted across the open foyer to the door of Grandfather's study. Putting my back against the firm wooden door, I ran my eyes over the deep shadows of the grand entryway. The only sound was the loud ticking of the big clock on the wall.

Satisfied, I pulled on the study door. It did not open. Reaching into my hair, I pulled out a bobby pin that held my straight hair out of my face. Crouching, I looked into the lock. I could see nothing. Inserting the bobby pin, I moved it carefully, listening and feeling for the tell-tale click that would tell me I was in.

The lock was old and bigger than the ones I was used to. I could feel myself starting to panic when the lock clicked.

I wilted against the door for a moment, giddy with relief. Trying the handle again, I found the door swung open easily. Testing the handle to ensure I could open it from the inside, I closed the door behind me, and moved across the room confidently. The moonlight that came through the sheer curtain covering the tall glass window was enough to light my way. Without hesitation, I went to Grandfather's desk and tried the first drawer. It slid open easily. Nothing of interest inside. Drawer after drawer and there was no sign of my dad's journal. I sat back on my heels to think. If Grandfather still believed the treasure was down in the canyons, he would not leave the journal lying around. I pulled out the drawers again, this time checking their length. The top one on the right side was shorter than the others. Pulling it out, I peered into the dimness. I pulled my flashlight out of my pocket and covered the lens with my hand. Clicking it on, I moved my index finger slightly to allow a narrow point of light to shine through the crack between my fingers into the space behind the drawer. It glinted off a keyhole in a narrow, wooden panel. Glancing around to ensure I was still alone, I tried the bobby pin. It was too big for the narrow opening. Turning off the light I bent the bobby pin open and used my teeth to remove the little rubber protective end. It was hard to manage the covered light and the bobby pin in the space of a single shallow drawer. Despite the cool of the night, I felt sweat running down my face. I had to have that book. My dad had been down in the mine. The picture in the book upstairs was proof. I had to have his journal if I was going to make any sense of the maze of caverns below. My frustration grew as the lock refused to respond to my probing.

Finally, I sat back to rest. Turning off the light, I sat in the dim moonlight. Dad had said God was always there, that He cared about me. It did not take much brains to figure out West's plan. Tomorrow morning they would call the trip off at breakfast making sure the news got around to all the staff.

Then, they would stage my running away to cover up their plan to take me by force to the mine. Laying back on the floor with my head close to the desk, I looked up through the thin curtains at the silvery moon.

"God, I need your help," I whispered. "You have always been my Dad's God. Dad said you would be my God too, if I let You. I want that. Would You help me get my dad's journal?"

My eyes drifted to the desk above me. I had to get that book. The center drawer of the desk was not shoved all of the way in. There was something reflective in that tiny crack. Reaching up, I slid the drawer out. There, tucked in a tiny leather band, tight against the back of the drawer, was a little silver key. I looked at it in disbelief. I would never have found it there. If the drawer had been shut, if the moonlight had not reflected off of the glossy cover of the book inside the drawer I had taken out. I touched the key above me. All of those things could be dismissed as chance or luck, but I knew better. I had prayed, and God had shown me the key.

I looked up at the moonlit sky. Could it be that God really did care about me? I had lived so many places where no one cared. But here, in a strange mansion, I had found friends almost instantly in my Grandfather's staff. And now, as if that were not enough, God had showed me the key that would probably save my life. I wiped my eyes and pulled the key free. Scrambling to my knees, I put it into the lock. It turned with a quiet click. Using a little ledge in the wood face, I pulled open the secret compartment. There, inside, was my Dad's journal along with several other folded papers and two of the pictures I had seen in the book. Tilting the pictures toward the moonlight, I could see that the blurry white patch was something on the canyon wall, not damage to the picture as I had thought before. I opened the other papers, they were Grandfather's and of no interest to me. I put them back into the secret drawer. The pictures were my dad's property so I slipped them inside his journal so I would not lose them along the way. I tucked my dad's journal into the waistband of my pajama pants. Pulling the string as tight as I could, I tied it in place. As long as I moved slowly, the book would not fall out. Just in case, I tucked the bottoms of my pant legs securely into my long socks. Replacing the wood face of the secret panel, I locked it into place. Sliding the key into its leather strap proved to be a challenge because the journal secured to my waist made bending much harder. I finally laid on the floor and reached up to put it away. I had just slid the last drawer into place when the office clock struck one. I gasped and felt like my heart had stopped completely.

It was good it had stopped, because a moment later the office door opened. I looked desperately around the room. The dark shadows behind the decorative couch were my only hope. I rose up enough to see over the desk. There was a dark figure in the doorway. He had not come all of the way into the room and seemed to be checking the entryway as I had done almost an hour before. Slipping the key back out of its place, and clutching the journal under my shirt, I crossed the open space in three quick steps to sink down awkwardly behind the couch. I was regretting my placement of the journal, but there was no time to move it.

As was becoming my custom, I peered out under the low couch and watched West's shoes cross the room to the desk. I recognized them instantly. He apparently knew right where the key was. His hand moved to the place, and he gave a soft angry exclamation. He was on his knees now, peering up where the key should have been. He stood facing the door, and I could see his long shadow that stretched across the floor silently shaking its fist. He searched half-heartedly for a few minutes before returning to the study door. He waited, listening, before disappearing into the darkness.

I gave him time to get away before moving from behind

the couch. Instead of putting the key back, I crouched and slipped it into the spine of a large book on the bottom shelf. Using my ruined bobby pin, I slid it deeper into the narrow crevice between the spine and the pages. There would be no disturbance in the dust.

Standing up, I adjusted my dad's journal to make sure it was secure. Making my way to the door, I waited as West had done. I had the eerie feeling I was being watched, but saw no one. Slipping out and across the entryway, I ran softly up the stairs to my room.

Holding the handle as I closed my door to keep the latch from clicking, I shone my flashlight quickly around the room. Nothing was out of place. I waited but could not sense any danger. The eerie feeling I had felt downstairs was gone. Moving to the bed, I pulled my carefully packed backpack from under it. Unloading the main section, I slid my dad's journal into a tear in the lining at the bottom of the bag, laying it as flat as possible against the thin plastic insert that gave the bag stability. I would have to pray West and Grandfather would not search it. As I reloaded the bag, putting in the beef jerky, batteries, light Jacket, and several other things I had requested or had been given over the last week, I thought about prayer. Lots of people said they would pray about stuff they either wanted or didn't want to happen. But maybe it wasn't praying that did it. Maybe it was like Dad said, that praying was just talking to God, and God was the one that did the doing. He had helped me find the key when I asked Him. Not because I prayed right, but because He knew what was best.

When everything was in place, I suddenly felt exhausted. It was one thirty. In five hours I would have to show up downstairs knowing my life could be in very great danger. I wished I had thought to try the phone in the office. I was tired enough now that I couldn't even remember if there had been a phone. I changed out of my pajamas into my jeans and a bright pink long sleeve shirt. It doesn't hurt to be visible when you are being kidnapped, I reasoned sleepily as I crawled into bed. I wrapped my arms around my backpack and slept.

# Chapter 9

"Polly? Polly are you awake?" Martha's voice blended with my hectic dreams. I was running away, trying to escape from West in the dark halls of the mansion. He grabbed me and started shaking me.

"Polly? Wake up sweetie. They are waiting for you downstairs."

In my dream, Martha's voice came out of West's mouth. My eyes popped open, and I blinked up at Martha who was standing over me.

"Are you okay? Do you feel alright?" Martha asked gently.

"I don't want to go to the mine anymore," I murmured.

She glanced back at my open bedroom door, "I think it is too late to change your mind now."

I sat up, clutching her arm, "If they say I ran away..." I fell silent at the sight of West looming in the doorway.

"Your grandfather said he had something important to tell you. He sent us to bring you down."

Martha's face did not agree with his statement, but she did not argue.

I got up and ran my brush through my hair. Now that I had two, I could keep the one Martha had given me out on the dresser.

"Can I braid my hair first?" I felt small and scared.

"There isn't time," West cut off whatever Martha was starting to say. "It is six thirty. Mr. Blossom has been waiting half an hour for you."

Slipping into the straps of my backpack, I picked up the pink hair ties I had laid out.

"Maybe there will be time after breakfast," Martha comforted as we followed West from the room.

"You can go back to your duties. I will see that she gets to the dining room," West informed Martha.

"I am coming with her," Martha spoke firmly and looked him in the eyes.

"Very well." West led the way down the stairs, staying close so he could overhear if we said anything he did not approve of.

When we entered the dining room, Grandfather was sitting in his place, his face hard with anger. "Did I not tell you 6 sharp?"

"Yes, Sir. I'm sorry. I forgot to set the alarm clock." I took my place meekly.

"Were you snooping around last night?" Grandfather demanded.

I looked as shocked as I felt. "Did someone else get hurt?" I looked over at Porter who had just entered with the platter of food. He too looked off his game this morning and did not even offer me a smile as he dished up my plate.

"No, something very important is missing," Grandfather answered.

"I think the house is scary at night," I told him truthfully. "Mr. West, were you up last night?"

He flushed angrily, and I did my best not to smile at his discomfort.

"West?" Grandfather turned on him. "Were you in my study last night?"

West stammered. He had not planned on facing an accusation and had not thought out a convincing answer.

Grandfather's thick eyebrows dropped lower. "I will

discuss this with you later."

West took his seat, sharing Grandfather's glowering mood.

It was Grandfather who broke the tense silence. "You are late." He was looking across at me. I shifted uncomfortably in my seat. His attention moved to West. "And you," he waved with disgust at his guest. "You are in my private study without my permission. I don't see what else I can do. The trip to the mine is cancelled."

I gaped at him. I had fallen right into his plan. My mind raced. There might be a chance that I could get to a phone before they staged my disappearance. Maybe I could get a message to one of the staff. I was staring at my food, thinking hard.

"No need to mope, child. Eat your breakfast. We can try again in a day or so." Grandfather's tone had lightened, and he seemed to have forgotten all about his missing key.

I forced myself to eat. If their plan worked, this could be my last real meal for a while.

"Porter, let the cooks know that we will not need a packed lunch," Grandfather directed. "The trip to the mine is off for today. We will eat here as usual."

With a little bow, Porter left to deliver the message.

Shivering at the cool way they were pulling off their plan, I shoved more eggs into my mouth. They seemed dry and tasteless. I forced them down with a drink of water, trying hard not to meet the cruel gaze of West.

"They say there is a lot of treasure hidden down in those caverns. No one knows where, but everyone agrees that it hasn't been found. Even your dad was looking for it, wasn't he?" West helped himself to more toast, buttering it liberally as he spoke. "Too bad the accident stopped him from finding it. He would have been famous, and you would have been a very rich young lady. Maybe you can find it when we go. And carry on his legacy."

West was droning on, but I was no longer listening. He had said "accident", but Grandfather had told me that my dad had gotten sick. Their stories didn't match, which meant they were covering up something important.

"Porter?" Grandfather's voice brought me back into the conversation. "I will need you to check the trail to the mine and ensure the warning sign at the end is still in place. I saw those boys on dirt bikes head out that way yesterday. Take the long trail, you might as well check that they did not tamper with the posted signs past the guest trail." He paused dramatically as if a thought had just occurred to him. "Take Polly with you. I won't have her pouting around the house trying to make everyone else miserable." He turned his attention to me. "You are not to go into the mine, do you understand? Stay with Porter. You are being punished for being inconsiderate and leaving us waiting for so long."

For a moment, I thought Porter would say no. He looked at Grandfather and West as if he did not trust either of them. The moment passed, and Porter left to make the necessary preparations.

"When I first came, you said I would not get to eat if I was late," I pointed out.

"I was only trying to help you be on time. I wouldn't actually make you skip a meal. You are a child, but you must still learn responsibility."

I nodded and finished my eggs. When I laid my napkin on the table, Grandfather cleared his throat and did the same. "Polly, go wait on the porch for Porter. He will bring the four wheeler around front and pick you up there."

Jane came in to collect the plates.

Not knowing what else to do, I shouldered my bag and went out to wait on the front steps. The steps my dad had laid with his own hands. I laid my hand on the even bricks. Why were they telling different stories about how dad died?

I needed to know what happened. I never even got to go to his funeral. Anger swelled in me. There was nothing I wanted to do more than run away from this place. I would have run right then if I had not known I would be making things easier for them if I did. And how far did I think I would get with a bright pink shirt on? I sighed. At least I would be with Porter. He would not let them hurt me.

————

Martha and Jane came out of the house followed closely by West.

I stood quickly, "I don't want to go to the mine."

"Don't be obstinate, Polly. We all know you are disappointed you couldn't go inside, but I promised you the other day that I would let you see the shaft before you went down. So, maybe this is a good thing after all." West pulled a paper from his pocket and handed it to Jane, "Do you mind picking me up a few things while you are in town?"

They hesitated, looking at me, but West stepped forward, blocking me from their sight as he dug in his pocket and produced a few folded bills which he placed with the list in her hand.

"That should cover the items I need," he said cheerily. "Even if we cannot go on the planned adventure, we can have a nice lunch together here on the grounds. Have a good trip."

There was no excuse to stay, so the ladies went to the waiting SUV and soon rumbled off down the drive. I saw a cloud of dust in the distance as they left the estate and turned onto the well-kept dirt road that led to town.

"There's no use pretending now," West told me. "Mr. Blossom is right. You need a lesson in responsibility before you can be trusted near a hazardous place like the mine shaft. You stay right with Porter and don't run off. Those hills can be dangerous."

I thought of the office again. Had there been a phone? I could not remember. I frowned. It wasn't like cell phones had not been invented. Why didn't anyone here carry one? I knew better than to ask West about it. Common sense would say that the retreat was too far from the city to get reception, so they didn't bother to carry phones that could not call. But there had to be a phone in the house. A landline like my grandmother had. With all the guests coming and going, there had to be a way to call out if there was an emergency.

"Maybe I should use the restroom before we go." I got up and headed into the house.

"Why not leave your backpack here with me?" West asked, eyeing it as if he had seen the glimmer of the missing key inside.

"No thanks, I'll take it with me." I opened the big door and went into the entryway. The study door was open, so I sauntered over to look inside. Grandfather was searching around the room for something.

"Grandfather, would you mind if I didn't go to check the sign with Porter? I'm not really up for the trip."

He straightened, annoyed at being found poking around in the couch cushions. "I don't care what you want, young lady. You have been nothing but trouble today. You were the one who was late. No doubt you were up in the night messing with things you haven't any business touching. Now something is lost, and I need time to look for it without having you underfoot."

This statement was ironic since the only time I saw Grandfather during the day was at meals or a rare sighting from a distance out on the grounds. I checked the desk. There was a very old fashioned phone. Maybe it was only made to look old. Suddenly it struck me that I had no one to call. I didn't know where my mom was. She changed phone numbers while I was at my uncle's, and he could never remember it when I asked. I didn't have a phone number for anyone else.

Grandfather followed my gaze and stepped in front of the phone. "You were instructed to wait out on the porch." Grandfather saw my bag and got the same greedy gleam I had seen in West's face a few minutes before.

"I came in to use the restroom," I told him. "What did you lose anyway? A dumb relic? I didn't take anything that belonged to you."

Turning away, I stalked off to the bathroom. My eyes felt hot and dry. There was no use crying about it. I was on my own now.

# Chapter 10

Porter was waiting on the four wheeler when I came out of the house. His face was hidden by the green helmet he wore. He had a smaller red helmet in his lap which he picked up and held out to me. When he didn't open the visor or speak, I hesitated. What if this wasn't Porter.

"You coming or not?" he asked, apparently unhappy with his assignment. Even muffled by the helmet, Porter's voice was unmistakable. I took the helmet and climbed on behind him. West came down the steps as if to say something, but Porter did not wait. He hit the gas and the four wheeler sprang forward and away from the distasteful man.

We went along the front of the house in the opposite direction of the gardens. It was no use trying to talk over the noise of the engine, so I focused on the scenery going by. Porter steered us off the driveway onto a narrow grassy trail that was slightly overgrown with weeds. We cut into the woods behind the house, following the winding trail towards the hills.

The Weatherbee Mine must have been a decoy, something to entertain the tourists while keeping them away from the actual entrance to the caverns.

I watched for landmarks as we went, in case I ever got to come back. The trail wound around so many trees that I quickly lost my bearing. I looked up at the sun through my visor. That at least would give me an idea of our direction as it was still on its initial upward arch from the east.

I was trying to watch, but my eyes were heavy. Last night's adrenaline and my wild dreams had left me very tired. The helmet seemed to pull my head forward as we crossed the gentle rocking rivets in the trail. My helmet rested against Porter's back, and I slept.

———

A deep rut in the trail jarred me, and I had to grab onto Porter to keep from losing my balance. He turned his head toward me, but I knew he couldn't actually see past the sides of his helmet. I didn't recognize anything. Looking back, I could see that we had left the main trail and were now bouncing down a less used, and very overgrown, path. Gripping handfuls of the back of Porter's loose Jacket to keep from falling off, I peered over his shoulder to see the trail ahead. At some point, rain had washed away portions of the ground leaving deep gashes in the earth that we jolted over at the same steady speed. I was grateful I'd worn jeans as the brush whipped against my legs. Every so often, I saw Porter's helmet turn for just a moment to the right or the left. After a few times, I was able to spot the posted signs he was looking for as we passed.

On and on we went, until my backside was sore. I was tense all over from the jarring, jerking ride when we pulled into a kind of clearing. It was overgrown like the trail, only the space between the trees gave away the fact that the land had once been cleared. One lone rock sat at the other end of the open space as if peering over the tall grass. I guessed that was the marker for the entrance of the mine.

"Here we are." Porter removed his helmet revealing his disheveled hair that was wet at the edges with sweat.

"This is the mine?" Letting go of his rumpled Jacket, I

looked around.

"Yes, but Mr. Blossom was pretty clear about staying away from that." The direction he looked confirmed my guess that the rock was at the entrance. Seeing my searching gaze was on the far end of the clearing, Porter pointed to the bent, metal "no trespassing" sign laying in the grass. It appeared to be well loved as if it was removed often. "There's the sign we are here to check." He got off the four wheeler taking the key with him. The simple action sent a tremor of fear through me.

I dismounted stiffly off the other side, putting a few feet between myself and Porter. The loose stones beneath the grass shifted under my feet.

He pulled the drill and screws from the compartment under the seat. A gentle breeze ruffled the grasses and the birds picked up their calls that our arrival had silenced. He sighed wearily and closed the compartment. "I guess we'd better get that sign back up where it belongs." Porter frowned a little, studying me. Staying where he was, he looked back slowly toward the mine as if expecting to see something. "Are you alright, Polly? You look like you saw something scary behind me." He looked back again, scanning the clearing. "Did you see someone?"

My gaze dropped to the key in his hand.

His frown deepened. "Seriously, Polly, are you okay? Was the ride too much for you? It is pretty rough in places, but the wheels can get stuck if I slow down too much. You look really pale. Maybe you should sit down."

"Why did you take the key?" I asked, my voice trembled. I knew I was overreacting, but this could be part of Grandfather's plan. Porter could go back and say there had been an accident.

"Wait, are you scared of me?" He stepped away as if to give me some space. "I thought we were looking out for each other." His eyes searched mine, trying to figure out the fear he seemed to be able to read in my face.

"Why did you take the key out of the four wheeler?" I asked again, nervously adjusting my backpack. Without transportation, I figured I could be lost for ages in these woods.

"I can only assume that there's a good reason behind your sudden distrust," Porter told me, picking up the last of the supplies he would need to fix the damaged sign. "I took the key out because if the pranksters who pulled down that sign are still hanging around, they would get a good laugh out of us having to walk back." He was watching me as if unsure if he should go fix the sign or try to keep me from fainting. "But there's a short way back that way," Porter pointed at the trees past the mine. "The main road is less than a mile away. So we'll be fine either way." He turned his attention back to me and frowned, his eyes searching mine for an explanation. "Polly, what's going on?"

"Porter, I think West and Grandfather are going to…"

"Put the drill down." Both of us jumped at the sound of West's voice. "So you came to the mine after all?" His tone was accusing.

"We came to fix the no trespassing sign like Mr. Blossom instructed." Porter moved closer to where I stood. "What are you doing here?"

"I'm here to ask you the same thing. Mr. Blossom trusted you to take care of Polly."

Porter's confused look melted into one of disgust. "It won't work, West. You and I both know it. Even if you put her down there, what good will it do you?"

"Me?" West's cold laugh set me on edge. "Don't be ridiculous, Porter. You are the one putting her down the shaft. If you follow my instructions, no one will get hurt." His eyes narrowed, "Put the girl down the shaft."

Porter's mouth opened, but West cut him off.

"I said, put her down." West commanded pulling out a gun. Something about the gun looked different. In the rush of fear my mind did not follow the fleeting thought.

I could see Porter was as scared as I was.

West's eyes were hard. "Either you put her down, or I'll shoot you. How long do you think you will last out here in the brush?"

"You can't shoot him!" I shouted. "The police will find you."

West laughed, "Only in the movies kid. You see, when I got here, Porter was trying to force you down the mine. I had to shoot him to save you. The story is easy to twist in my favor. What will it be, Porter?"

"I'm not putting her down that shaft, West," Porter faced him squarely. "You can shoot me if you want. I'm not putting her down there to die."

I watched as Porter's gaze dropped to the gun in West's hand. A moment later, a look of understanding came into his face.

"That's a tranquilizer gun, isn't it? That's what you did to Mason." Porter was putting the pieces together as he spoke. "I knew the accident was fake. That tranquilizer gun was the missing clue. We all knew Mason was too good on a four wheeler to go off a ravine like that. You lost your temper and hit Mason one too many times, didn't you? You knew a stunt like that would land you back in jail, so you tranquilized him, put him on the four wheeler and pushed it over the cliff."

"Too bad your accusations will die with you," West scoffed. I could see a hint of pride in his gleaming eyes. "I have a score to settle and don't have time to waste."

"You can kill me for all I care. I'm not hurting Polly." Porter stood straight and tall, his face stoic.

"Now, now, I don't want anyone to get hurt, especially not Polly," West reassured him with a cruel smile. "That treasure is down there, and she happens to be little enough to get through the shaft. I'll pull her back up when she finds it."

"And then what?" Porter challenged.

# Chapter 11

Suddenly, what Porter had said about my dad sunk in. West had killed my dad. It wasn't an accident or a sickness, West had met my dad out here, and there was a fight. What it was about didn't matter now. West had shot him with some kind of sleeping dart and staged an accident to cover his tracks.

"You killed my dad!" I shouted. "You killed him in cold blood and got away with it. That's why I didn't get to go to the funeral. That's why I've been shuffled around like a bad card." I was so angry that I could hardly see straight. "You took my dad away. He was the only one who loved me." I grabbed a handful of loose stones from the ground to hurl at him.

Porter grabbed my arm and pulled me back. I fought him, angry tears blinding me.

"Polly, you losing it now won't help your dad." Porter's voice was calm. He turned my hand over and pried it open so the stones fell out. "We have to stick together, Polly. We have to keep our cool." He slipped something into my hand, and I knew instantly that it was the key to the four wheeler. Closing my fingers around the key, he put his hands around my closed fists. Looking me in the eyes, he added softly, "I'll do everything I can to keep you safe."

I nodded. Shooting a glare at West to show I had not forgotten, I shoved my fists into my pockets. The key was safe for now.

"That was very touching." West's words were dripping with sarcasm. "Too bad. You were such a good butler. But then, it is usually the butler who is behind the crime in the movies, isn't it, Polly?" West came toward us.

"If he puts me down the mine, will you let him go?" I wiped my eyes with the sleeve of my shirt.

"Of course," West lied.

"Alright, you let him go and I will go down the mine."

"Look who is calling the shots now." West's smile was condescending. "No, Polly, I will shoot Porter if he does not put you down. Then I will put you down myself. It will not be hard to convince the authorities that it was Porter who put you down before he had his terrible accident on the four wheeler. It all depends on if you want to see him die before you go in."

"West, let her go," Porter was not pleading. "You can't get away with this. Even if the treasure is down there, it won't do you any good without me here. You know that."

West's eyes narrowed, and Porter fell silent.

I stepped away from them. "If you are going to kill Porter either way, what is the use of doing what you say? Why shouldn't I just run off into the woods?" I challenged.

It looked as if the big man was genuinely amused. "If you run, little girl, I'll slow you down with one of my darts, take care of Porter here, and drop you in the mine like a pebble in a pool. Either way, you won't come up until you find that treasure."

There was no use arguing. I had thought of the fact that West could easily shoot me before I could get out of sight. "I will have to go into the mine." I whispered, looking across at the rock.

Porter knelt and looked up into my face. "Polly, you have what it takes to foil his plan."

For a moment, I stared at him blankly. My mind trying to grasp what he was saying.

"Polly, I don't care what he does to me. You have to be strong." Porter was looking into my eyes, willing me to understand. "The caverns are dangerous and unmapped. No one even knows if the treasure is actually down there."

Suddenly, it clicked. I had the key. Without the four wheeler key, West could not stage Porter's death. The police would be able to see there was foul play and would trace it back to him.

Porter gave me a little smile, he knew I understood. Even if he died, West would not get away with it like he had with my dad. He would go to prison and not be able to hurt anyone else. The only chance was for me to go down in the mine with the four wheeler key. There would be no way West could stage an accident if he could not start the vehicle. Once I was safely out of West's reach, Porter would have a fighting chance. "You have to put me down. Please Porter, I don't want to see you die."

"Alright, enough of this," West grabbed Porter by the shoulder of his jacket and pulled him up and away from me.

Porter's arm whipped around, knocking West's hand from his shoulder. West jumped back, keeping the gun out of Porter's reach. They stood glaring at each other for several seconds.

West took another step back, keeping the tranquilizer gun pointed at Porter. "If you do not have her in the shaft in the next thirty seconds, I will shoot you and do it myself." His tone was low and angry.

We could both see he was not bluffing.

"It's stupid to tell me I have to go down without telling me where it is." I grabbed at the earth and threw a clod of dirt at him which he dodged easily. "I'll find your dumb treasure and come back to haunt you. You are a murderer and will pay for what you have done. Porter, put me down the mine, now." I stormed towards the rock and the mine entrance. I couldn't afford to have West stop me or search my bag.

"Twenty-four seconds." West told Porter with an amused look.

"Polly, please." Porter followed, I could hear the swish of the grass behind me. If we seemed too eager, West would get suspicious.

"Where is the shaft?" I demanded, sorry our last interaction had to be like this.

Porter felt around in the dirt until he found the corner of a board. With a grunt, he slid it out of the way, revealing a hole in the ground which looked to be a little narrower than my shoulders.

Porter looked over at West.

"How do I get down?" I asked, shoving my hands into my pockets. My fingers closed around the key. I would throw it down the shaft if needed. I would have all the time in the world to find it again once I was down there.

"There's a nice bucket elevator you get to ride," West told me as if I was a clueless four year old. To Porter he said, "Reach inside, you will find a chiseled out indent with a wooden peg. The rope is coiled on that."

"Polly, please don't make me do this," Porter knelt and felt around in the dark shaft for the rope.

Keeping my back to West, I took the key from my pocket, kneading my closed fist nervously. I slid my backpack from my back and slipped the key inside between the zippers as I pretended to peer down the hole.

While I was doing this, Porter pulled up a thick coil of rope. On the end, was a large bucket nearly the size of the hole itself. It made sense, I told myself. If someone was putting down supplies, it would be silly to use a small container. The hole had to be very deep to need so much rope. As soon as the bucket neared the top, I dropped my bag into it. Porter let go of the rope and the bucket hurtled downward.

"I didn't say she could take the bag!" West surged forward, but changed his mind, as if he did not want to get too close to Porter at such a delicate stage of his plan. "Pull it back up."

Porter made what looked like an effort to stop the rope by stepping on the coil. The rope jerked and we heard a clang of metal and a muffled thump below.

The rope swung lightly. It was so hard not to look at Porter. I knew he too felt the pride of the small victory. Somehow he had managed to get the bucket to hit the side on the way down, dumping my backpack in its final jerk at the bottom. My backpack, and the key, were safely at the bottom of the shaft.

When the bucket came up out of the darkness, it was empty. West muttered angrily, but there was nothing he could do about it. "Put the girl down, now." He ordered through clenched teeth.

Without being told, Porter put his hand around the thick rope attached to the bucket handle. Keeping it tight, he looked across at the trees moving sideways a little as if aligning himself with some unseen marker. Satisfied, Porter took one solid step away from the mine. Stooping, he moved some stones, uncovering a low C shaped piece of metal that came out of the rock.

I watched him closely. It was apparent that this was not the first time he had done this. Had he sent supplies down this hole before to my dad? The pictures in the book proved that Dad had been down there, but even I could see the hole was too narrow for my dad. I wasn't even sure I would fit. There had to be another entrance. A secret one only my dad knew about. Was the secret entrance the reason West had killed him?

Porter hooked the rope behind the loop, keeping it taut

so the bucket remained at the mouth of the shaft. He moved into position so he could let the rope out gradually. Looking at me, Porter nodded. "Be careful."

I knew my flashlight was packed well and would not have been damaged, but I decided to take my last chance to get another.

"Mr. West, do you have a flashlight?" I asked timidly.

"Why? Are you scared of the dark?" he taunted.

"It looks awfully deep." I did not have to try to sound concerned. I peered into the hole. Once I was inside, and the rope was coiled again, there would be no way for me to get back out of the mine.

I turned to West, who waited impatiently. "How will I find the treasure without a light?"

My mind was racing. If I could fasten a string to the bucket, I might be able to pull it off the peg and down to me. I had a flat spool of thin, sturdy woven string in my bag below. Would I be able to find it and tie it to the bucket before it was pulled back up?

West held out a small, thin metal box to me. It had a single button on one side and a purse-like strap was attached to the narrow end. "Take this down into the caverns with you. When you find the treasure, push the button, and it will send me a signal." I reached out to take it, and he held onto it. "Each time you push the button without the treasure, I will remove one of Mr. Blossom's staff, your so called friends, from the retreat. This is not a game."

I nodded seriously.

He released the box, and I put it around my neck and arm so the strap hung across my chest. He handed me a small flashlight and gestured to the mine. "It is all yours!"

I bit my lip to keep back my fear. Moving to the edge of the shaft, I placed my feet one at a time into the bucket. It was a tight fit, but I would be able to stand in the bucket as

I was lowered into the mine.

"Porter, did my dad really die?"

He looked surprised but kept lowering. "Yes."

"You saw him?" I had to know.

It looked as if the memory was painful, and, for a moment, I did not think he would answer.

"I did."

I nodded. For years I had clung to the hope that Dad was only hiding away. Now I knew it was not true.

"Keep your eyes open, and watch the walls," Porter instructed cryptically.

"Okay," I answered, not sure yet what he meant. I stood, allowing the bucket to hold my weight as I slid downward into the dark hole.

"No talking," West ordered sharply.

As we had done so many times in the dining room, we smiled with our eyes, secret friends who would stand up for each other in a pinch. The bucket moved smoothly. I felt the cool of the earth settle over me as the shaft rose above me on all sides. Suddenly, as if it were grabbing me, the shaft narrowed around me. I felt the bucket moving away from beneath my feet. For an instant, panic gripped me like the walls of the shaft. Porter must have felt the difference in the tension of the rope, he paused, giving me time to wriggle through the narrow place. After that, the shaft opened up a little, and the rough stone walls were somehow comforting. They were my last contact of the sun warmed earth. I gripped the rope, looking up to watch the sunlit opening move away.

Remembering that I wouldn't have much time to secure the string to the bucket, I forced myself to look down into the darkness. I would need for my eyes to be adjusted to the darkness if I wanted to succeed. I could see nothing below. Only blackness that seemed to swallow everything. I prayed as I was lowered down. I prayed for Porter, that God would not let West kill him. I prayed for West to get caught. For myself, that…I did not know what to pray. That I would find the treasure? It did not seem important anymore. I had seen too many people hurt by others who are only looking out for themselves. I thought of my mom. As far as I knew, she was a part of this treasure hunt. Parents are people too. People, just grown up kids, who get to choose if they will do right or wrong. People who have been hurt and who sometimes never learn to think about others instead of themselves. I probably would have turned out just like her. Always seeking the next pleasure, always thinking about my own happiness, if it hadn't been for my dad. When he gave his life to Jesus, he changed. Not just how he acted, but even who he was changed. He helped me see that there was another way to live.

Letting go of the rope with one hand, I pulled out the light West had given me, half expecting it not to work. When I pressed the button, it came on instantly. Scanning the smooth rocks below, I located my backpack. I knew right where the string was, but I would have to get it before Porter pulled up the bucket. I knew West was impatient and on edge.

"God, I'm really scared right now," I prayed. "Please help me get this bucket tied so I can get back up there and see the sun again."

Holding the flashlight in my mouth, I leaned down from the bucket and grabbed my bag.

Porter must have felt the change because I felt him hesitate through the rope.

He was lowering me again, but much slower than before. Hooking my elbow around the rope I scrambled to get the spool of string from my bag. Letting the backpack fall, I frantically tied the cord to the handle of the bucket. Knot after knot, trying hard to remember how to tie one that would not come undone. The bucket stopped just above the rock floor, and I stepped out, giving the sturdy string one last pull to snug the bumpy row of knots that my life depended on.

The bucket started to rise, slowly. Porter was giving me more time. My light glinted off a piece of chipped quartz, and I tossed it into the bucket. I wasn't sure why I did it. I suppose it was one last gift for Porter. One last connection.

I looked up at the uneven circle of light high above me. The bucket swung gently, eclipsing the light. And sometimes blocking it all together. Emotion welled over me.

"God, please protect Porter," I whispered.

# Chapter 12

Porter took his time coiling the rope and hanging it and the metal handle of the big bucket on their peg. With it hanging there, the circle of sunlight at the top of the shaft looked like the kind of thick crescent moons kids draw. I thought I saw Porter wave, silhouetted by the sunlight, but he was so high above me that I could not be sure. I had let the string play through my hand as the bucket went up. I could only hope that the wave from Porter meant he had seen it and coiled the rope so I could pull it back down.

I waited, listening hard.

"You were supposed to keep the key, Polly," Porter called down. His silhouette reached into the bucket, and he scrambled to his feet knocking a few pebbles down the shaft. I jumped out of the way as they came raining down. Grabbing my bag, I dumped it frantically on the ground. Digging through my supplies I found the four wheeler key and sat back on my heels. What had Porter meant? I could hear muffled voices above me, indistinct and angry. Porter was back at the mouth of the shaft and West must have followed him because I could now hear him going on about finding the key.

"I threw it that way," Porter said matter-of-factly. He was speaking loudly to West as if he wanted me to hear it too. "Go look for it if you want it, Mr. West." The way Porter said 'mister' was anything but polite. "You've lost your advantage, and you know it. Polly is safe, and you don't have the key. It was so easy to stage it as an accident last time that you forgot to think this one out. Let this one go, West. If you hang on much longer, you won't be able to back out." Porter's silhouette blocked the light almost completely. "Happy hunting, Polly." Porter called down cheerily. His voice echoed through the hollow rock passageways, making them feel somehow friendly. The cover was moved into place, shutting out the light and West's angry shouts.

Even with my light, the darkness closed in around me. It's cold breath whispering across my face. I turned off the flashlight and stood in the blackness for several minutes. I wasn't sure exactly what I was waiting for, a gunshot or something like that, I suppose.

Clicking on my flashlight, I pulled my dad's journal and the other papers out of my bag. Setting them aside, I put my dumped belongings back into my backpack. Once that was done, I sat cross-legged on a rock shelf to think. I turned off the light again. I would need it more when I was moving through the mine.

Porter had made it look like I had sent the key up to him. He must have thrown that piece of quarts making West think it was the key. He was protecting me. Porter knew that if West found out that I had the key, he would start threatening me to get me to send it up. He had already threatened to hurt Miss Ella, Jane, and Martha.

Hugging my knees to my chest, I rested my chin on them. Why did Porter care what happened to me? He barely knew me, and there was nothing special about me to make him care. Most people treated me like I was a bother, but Porter had been kind from the start. I looked up toward the shaft. There was the faintest light far above that could not reach into the darkness where I sat. Yet it seemed like that faint light had worked its way into my heart. It was not enough to push back the hurts of my past, or take away the fear I felt now, but somehow, that tiny glimmer of hope had made its way inside me. Someone actually cared about me. He had known my dad, and my dad had been his friend. I scrambled to my feet, knowing what I had to do.

I could no longer hear anything from above. Clicking on my flashlight, I looked around. If West was still up there, I couldn't afford to let him get his hands on my Dad's journal. Flashing the light around, I discovered that the shelf I had sat on had a good amount of room underneath. I was shoving my backpack into the space when it occurred to me that the floor was smooth. Water might come through here if there was a heavy rain. Even though I knew now it was an excuse, Grandfather had delayed my trip into the mine because of the rain. The last thing I needed was for the journal to get wet.

Again, I searched the rounded stone cavern. The orange layers would be fun to examine if I had more time. A rock ledge above me cast a dark shadow upward on the rough wall. There were enough uneven places that I knew I would be able to scale the few feet up to the ledge. I had a better light in my backpack, but I might need it later.

Moving carefully, and still listening for sounds from above, I made my way up to the low ledge. Getting my backpack off while clinging to the narrow finger ledge required more skill than I had. This meant I had to climb back down and remove one strap. I glanced up at the faint light at the top of the shaft. I was wasting precious time. It could mean life or death to Porter. When I climbed up again, my progress was much quicker. I knew what handholds to grab and where to put my shoes. Climbing past the ledge, I slid my bag onto the rock and shoved it back until it was securely wedged. Satisfied, I scrambled down.

Hurrying back to the bottom of the shaft, I located the string and gently, but steadily, pulled it downward. At first it did not move. I shone my light up but could not make out anything except the dim shine of the bottom of the bucket.

"God, please help this to work. Porter needs me," I prayed aloud, my voice echoing in the darkness. Steady. I had to keep the pressure steady. The string grew tighter and tighter as I slowly drew it downward. Something above me popped. For an instant, I thought my string had broken. The next moment, I was aware of a movement above and instinctively dove out of the way of the incoming bucket. It stopped with a sharp jerk, dangling just inches from the stone floor.

Picking myself up from the floor, I rubbed my sore elbow. Pulling up my sleeve, I was not surprised to see it was skinned but nothing serious. The bucket was swinging as if caught in a gentle breeze. Not stopping to check for other injuries, I went to the bucket and stepped inside. I shoved the flashlight deep into my back pocket so the light shown upward, leaving my hands free. I would have to climb the rope to get out. Taking a deep breath, I gripped the rope and pulled myself up. My feet found the bucket handle and I shoved myself higher on the rope. Holding my place with my tennis shoes, I moved my hands up and pulled again. Getting to the top was not optional. Whatever West had done to Porter, I had to help him. Higher and higher I went. My arms were trembling now. The shaft was narrowing around me. More and more often, my elbows and knees knocked painfully against the stone walls. It did not matter. My mom was a quitter, but I didn't have to be. I didn't have to live off of other people. I would take responsibility and give back.

My feet slipped, and I clung desperately to the rope. I would have to keep my mind on the task at hand, or I wouldn't live to help anyone. Bracing my feet against one side of the shaft, I pushed my back against the other side. Still holding the rope loosely, I rested my hands for a few seconds. Peering up to the weak light that slipped through under the shaft cover above. I was only half way there.

"You are half way, Polly," I whispered to myself. "Porter needs you. Keep going."

Having the wall to brace against helped. Now, instead of using only the rope, I could push with my feet against the walls of the shaft to help move myself upward. I remembered the tight spot up near the top and smiled. That would be helpful if I could reach the cover from there.

Now and then, my foot would slip, and my shoulders or elbows would hit the unforgiving walls of the shaft. Once I lost my footing and fell. My arm connected solidly with the uneven shaft wall as I spread out, grasping for anything in my attempt to stop myself. I clung there, bracing and panting.

Taking a deep breath, and ignoring the pain, I grabbed the rope once more. Shoving myself upwards again and again. My legs and arms were shaking with the effort. I imagined my dad lying dead under the crashed four wheeler and pushed on fiercely. I had to try to save Porter.

After what seemed like forever, I reached the narrow portion of the shaft. Here it was only wide enough for the mouth of the bucket to pass through. I remembered having to draw in my shoulders to fit on the way down. Reaching through, I gripped the rope as high as I could. Squirming upwards, I twisted, pulled, and pushed myself through to the other side. Here the shaft widened again. I wondered briefly if the narrow portion was made up of a more dense rock layer that stood up better against the original drilling or digging of the vent shaft. It must have been what the shaft was for when it was made. Whatever it was made of, it wasn't going anywhere, and next year I would be too big to squirm through into the mine.

Bracing my feet against the sides, I put my hands against the cover and pushed against it. It moved slightly. I set my feet once more. Pushing against the wood to lift up one side, I managed to slide it about a foot to the left. Blinding sunlight enveloped me with warmth. One more push, and the cover was out of the way! I shaded my eyes against the light. Moving up where I could see out, I scanned the clearing. There was no sign of West or Porter. The birds I had startled hesitantly resumed their cheerful banter. I scrambled up and out to lay panting on the warm grass.

There was no time to rest, my muscles protested as I got to my feet. Looking around the clearing, I got my bearings. The four wheeler was still there. West would return for it. Turning back to the mine entrance, I dragged the cover back into place. There would be no evidence that I had emerged. Now to find Porter!

I stood quietly, listening for any sound that would indicate what direction they had gone. The bright sunlight and birds chirping cheerily seemed out of place. How could things be happy when someone could be dying? I thought of my dad and decided against that. I would deal with those emotions later. Porter needed me now. Only I had no idea where to find him. I found a grassy spot and knelt on my sore knees. I folded my hands like I had seen kids in books and pictures do when they prayed, and closed my eyes.

"God, thank you for getting me out of that mine," I said softly, feeling awkward praying aloud in the woods. "I don't really know how to ask You, but if it isn't too much trouble, could you help me find Porter before it is too late? And could You help me get him to safety or send someone to help him?" I started to get up, and then added, "Amen". That was how they did it on movies. Mom didn't like me to go to church, but she let Dad take me a few times. People in church said 'amen' after they prayed. I knew God was the one who got to pick if something got done, but this was important, and in case it mattered, I wanted to do it right.

When I opened my eyes, there before me was a clear line of crushed grass. Something heavy had been dragged this way. I would never have noticed it from where I had been standing.

Scrambling up, I followed the fresh trail. It was where West had dragged Porter. It had to be. My eyes darted from the crushed grass to the edges of the woods and back again. The last thing I wanted to do was to run into West now. A movement ahead caused me to crouch quickly behind some scraggly bushes. A doe stepped out silently, she too was scanning the clearing for danger. I was about to continue my search when the deer's head jerked up. Her attention was turned away from me. She was watching something at the edge of the clearing ahead of me. In a flash, she darted into the safety of the trees. I waited and was rewarded by the crunch of boots coming toward me.

I crouched lower.

"Why is the four wheeler still here?" Grandfather's stern voice came from behind me.

Why had I worn bright pink? I flattened myself against the warm dirt thankful for the tall grass around me. I could only hope that if I could not see them, I was also hidden from their view.

"Porter tossed the key off into the brush. It will be impossible to find," West answered, his voice coming closer. He was the one that had frightened the doe.

"Not for the police. A trained dog will pick up that key in a matter of minutes." Grandfather was upset, I knew the tone well. "What were you thinking?"

"Look, the girl is down the mine, and Porter is out of the way," West pointed out. "If you want to dig around for the key, be my guest. I say we leave it here and let the police know the four wheeler and Porter are both missing." West and Grandfather were past me now. It sounded like they were on the other side of the grassy area. I kept my head down just in case.

"He took the girl out to repair the sign, and this is how we found things," West continued calmly. "Porter must have told her he was putting her down the shaft, and she tossed the key to get even. He forced her down the shaft and walked off the cliff when he recklessly tried to flee the scene of the crime."

I could almost hear West smiling with satisfaction.

"And the trail through the grass where you dragged him?" Grandfather asked, skeptically.

"Don't worry about it. I saw that I was leaving a trail through the grass before I reached the edge of the clearing. I carried him the rest of the way. It fits with our story. Porter had to drag her back to the mine entrance when she tried to get away," West explained.

"I don't know if they will buy it, but it is at least feasible," Grandfather agreed half-heartedly.

I heard their feet crunching through the grass away from me.

"How will the girl alert you if she finds the treasure?" Grandfather asked.

I felt my face crinkle with disgust when Grandfather referred to me as "the girl" as if I had no name.

"I gave her a radio transmitter. But don't worry, it cannot connect to an actual radio," West assured him. "It will ping the receiver I have set up at the lodge. The cell signal is too weak at the lodge to make use of any other method. But I may be able to track her progress through the caverns with the signal. That will lead us to the entrance Hamilton was using."

So that was his plan. The first thing I would do after I got Porter to safety would be to get rid of that transmitter.

"And she knows how to use it?" Grandfather did not sound convinced.

"It's a single button, Mr. Blossom. I'm sure she's got enough brains to figure it out."

The crunching stopped. "Watch yourself, West," Grandfather warned. "You are in this too deep to get cocky with me."

West must have backed down because they continued on out of the clearing. I raised myself on my elbow, risking one quick look to confirm they were headed toward the road Porter had mentioned. Easing myself back down, I waited until I could no longer hear them. My heart was pounding, and the adrenaline kept me alert. The birds resumed their calling, signaling the strangers had left the area. Slowly I raised myself once more. There was no sign of West or Grandfather. I got to my knees and looked around. Nothing. Moving carefully, I followed the trail of crushed grass to where it stopped a few feet away from where I had been hiding. Now, I had to be more attentive. A broken stick, grasses pressed down, any of them could be the marks of an animal. Or, they could be the trail of a killer.

A boot print in a patch of sand caught my eye. Moving forward more quickly, I found the place where West had forced his way through the bushes. I went carefully. If there was a cliff, the last thing I wanted to do was go hurtling off of it.

# Chapter 13

I was so focused on picking up West's trail that I walked right into a patch of thorny vines. I looked around for the best way out. A few steps ahead was a rock, I could see nothing past it. That was the edge of the cliff! Spotting a place where the vines thinned out, I moved in that direction, gingerly pulling the thorns from my arms and legs as I backed out of the tangle. Skirting the brush, I ducked under the low branches of a tree and crawled forward to the rocky edge of the cliff.

Why hadn't anyone tried to dig through to the canyons here? The drop off was steep, and it seemed like it would be simple to bore through the rocky face to get to the tunnels inside. I wondered about this as I picked my way downward to keep my mind off of finding Porter's body among the rocks. Mentally, I selected the deep crevices where I would have dug through if I had been a miner wanting to find the treasure inside the caverns beneath the earth.

West had mentioned my dad's entrance. I wondered where it could be. If Dad was getting into the mine and Porter was sending down supplies, Dad must have found the treasure. I knew the journal would hold the truth. If Grandfather had it, he must have gotten it from West or my dad's room at the resort after Dad was killed.

I was a good way down the cliff now, but had to stop to rest. My arms were still feeling like jelly after my climb up the shaft rope. At least this was downhill. Looking around, I realized that this was not an actual cliff. It was a deep ravine. Trees and brush grew up between the rocks blocking my view, but I could make out a winding dirt trail at the bottom of the steep valley. Holding on to a tree branch to keep my balance, I stood shakily on a rock that jutted out a foot or so and gave me a decent view of my side of the rocky incline. My eyes moved over the boulders below. There was no sign of Porter. I tried to remember what he had been wearing. A dark Jacket over a... It had been zipped and, in the rush of emotions, I had not noticed what color shirt he had been wearing. It didn't matter anyway, the Jacket would hide it. But he had been wearing blue jeans. Surely those would be visible from here. Again and again I moved my eyes systematically over the rocks as if I were trying to find a letter in a crossword puzzle. Nothing. Not even a hint of blue anywhere.

No one could survive a fall like this! I chided myself for thinking it, but knew it was true. If Porter had fallen to where I was…My eyes darted upward even before my mind could finish the thought. There were trees and brush everywhere, and West would have been in a hurry to get rid of the evidence. If he tossed Porter over, maybe, just maybe, there was a chance that Porter didn't actually fall.

I searched desperately, wishing I could see through the trees. Praying I would find him while hoping without hope that he had somehow gotten away. Then I saw it, protruding from behind a rock, only three or four feet from the top of the ridge was a brown boot and the blue jean color that had caught my eye. It was Porter. I stood there as if glued to the rock. I was so afraid of what I would see. I remembered Porter's expression when I had asked him if he had seen my dad after he was killed. Things like this are not easily forgotten.

What would I do when I reached him? I could not carry him up the rocks alone, and if I went down, we would both end up crushed at the bottom.

A sound worked its way into my consciousness and I looked down. A lean figure on a dirt bike went by below me. I screamed for help. My voice echoed back to me sounding weak and pitiful. I knew he could not hear me over the noise of his bike. I looked back and saw two more boys coming down the winding trail towards the ravine. I had to get their attention.

Grabbing a bunch of grass at its roots I jerked hard, almost knocking myself down into the gully when the whole bunch came up from its shallow bed in one piece. I looked back, the first boy had been far ahead of the others, but I knew I was quickly losing time. I grabbed another bunch of weeds and pulled. Bracing for the moment the roots would release their hold, I managed to keep my balance when the plant came up in my hand.

Plopping the two grass bunches on the rock I was standing on, I wedged a fist-sized stone in where the grass was the thickest just by the roots. That would give it more weight and hopefully make it fly further. Standing with one grass bunch in each hand, I hurled the first one downward towards the path. My throw was off, and the clump fell short, but it did spray the first rider with dirt. Only one more chance. I pressed the stone further in and threw it hard. The grass flew root first, landing a few feet in front of the last rider. He swerved and stopped his bike just out of my line of sight. I could tell by the change in the sound of his engine, but the thick foliage of a tree hid him from sight.

"Help!" I screamed over and over. I could only hope West and Grandfather had gone back to the resort. I was frantically jerking up grass clods and hurling them down toward the trail, not even bothering to add stones. Tears came from nowhere making it hard to see. Desperation gripped me, and I let go of the supporting branch of the tree. Nothing mattered now except getting help for Porter.

Something hit me, showering me with dirt. I blinked hard to get it out of my eyes.

"At least now you know how it feels." A young man's voice broke the sudden stillness. "What's the matter with you anyway? You lost?"

"He's hurt bad," I blubbered. "I think he is, but I don't know."

The teen pulled out a walkie-talkie and pressed the side button. "Jamal, Robert, better get back here. I've got a crazy girl who says someone is hurt."

His radio crackled. "Where are you, Jake?"

"Up the ravine on the rock side, part way up to the Forgotten Mine shaft." Jake responded through the radio.

"Be right there."

Jake turned to me. "What was the idea of throwing dirt clods at me?" he demanded. "I was coming up to help you."

"I didn't see you." I wiped my eyes on my sleeve and realized the cloth was torn.

"I guess not with the way you were blubbering." His tone shifted, and he observed with more sympathy, "You got a pretty nasty cut on your arm."

"Porter is up there. I think he is hurt. West meant to kill him," I blurted wiping my eyes again on my other sleeve which was still intact. "I can't carry him alone." Once my eyes were clear, I could see the teen was about two feet taller than me. His sandy blond hair was damp with sweat. When I saw the mud sprayed on his front, it made sense why they were riding so far apart.

"Porter? Like Mr. Blossom's man?" Jake asked looking around. "Where?"

"He's up there. I found him just before I heard your bikes."

"Robert, meet us at the top. Porter is up there. She says he's hurt bad." Jake did not wait for me. He started scrambling up the rocks like a mountain goat.

"Over to your right, behind the big boulder below that pine tree." I called up, trying to catch up with him. Jake altered his course slightly to the right.

Watching him, I missed my footing, and my shin connected solidly with the edge of a rock. I sucked my breath in sharply, forcing myself to keep going.

Jake was to Porter now.

I hesitated, fearful.

"He's alive, but pretty banged up. Looks like he took a beating or bounced off of a couple of these rocks on the way down," Jake called. "Do you have anything to stop the bleeding?"

I rounded the boulder and gasped. Porter was sprawled face up on the rocks. His face was bruised, and it was hard to see where the blood on his face had come from. Wherever it came from, there was a lot of it.

"Heads bleed a lot," Jake informed me. "It could be just a little split somewhere. I'm not a doctor but the face scratches don't look bad to me."

West probably got tangled in those thorns up there and tossed Porter over. I could imagine him, angrily facing the thorns I had stumbled into myself.

"Oh, here it is. See, his head is bleeding there where the hair is matted." Jake continued. "Blows to the head can be dangerous. I'm afraid moving him could hurt him worse."

"If you have a knife, you could use my sleeves to stop the bleeding," I offered.

Jake looked up at me, and I saw a hint of admiration in his eyes. "You are pretty tough for a kid." He dug in his pocket and handed me his pocket knife.

"You better do it," I said, pushing it back toward him. "I'll cut my arm off."

He laughed and I slipped my arm out through the gaping

tear above my elbow. Pulling my torn sleeve away from my arm, Jake cut through it and folded it into a makeshift pad.

"Come around here and hold it against his head," Jake instructed.

I moved around him, he caught my hand to steady me when I slipped.

"Sorry," I mumbled. Crouching between the rocks near Porter's head, I gently pressed the cloth against the oozing cut. "Better do the other sleeve," I instructed. "This one isn't going to be enough." I glanced up to see Jake studying me. "I can't cut it off and hold this one on," I told him bluntly.

"You are a strange kid."

"Stop calling me a kid," I ordered. There wasn't time to waste on observing how messed up I was. Enough people had done that already. "My name is Polly. If you want to call me something you can call me that."

He suppressed a smile and set to work on my other sleeve. I had a Jacket in my backpack so I would be fine without sleeves in the mine.

"I would use my own shirt, but it is pretty nasty," Jake apologized. He slipped the detached portion of my left sleeve from my arm and folded it up for me so I would not have to take the pressure from Porter's head wound. I added the second cloth and pressed gently.

"You called your friends on the walkie-talkie. Can you call out for help?" I asked. "West will be back any time to make it look like Porter's fall was an accident."

Jake grabbed the radio and held it to his mouth, "Jamal, send Robert up with the medical kit. You get on your bike and go for help."

"Not to the resort," I hissed.

Jake nodded. "Stay away from the Resort. Go to Old Man Johnson's place. Have him get an ambulance."

"You could have told me that before I climbed up here,"

Jamal said from behind us, panting from the effort of the climb. He was dark skinned and thicker than Jake. Wiping the sweat from his forehead onto his pants, he looked over at me. "I'm Jamal."

I had met lots of hard faced teens over my lifetime and quickly learned which ones to avoid. Even though these guys were four or five years older than me, beneath their muddy, adventurous appearance there was something gentle and real about them that made me feel safe.

"Robert, do you read me?" Jake asked into the radio. He looked at me and added, "He gets ahead sometimes and goes out of range. He might still be riding."

A voice over the radio interrupted him. "I'm closer to the bikes, so I'll go for help. I'll leave the medical kit on Jamal's bike."

"You go get it," Jamal told Jake.

I was surprised when Jake stood and headed down the rocks without protest.

Jamal noticed my reaction. "He's quicker on the rocks, and I've had some medical training. My dad is an EMT. It's a little town, so the Emergency Medical Technicians are also the firemen as needed. I volunteer with them, but I can't officially join until I'm 18." While he spoke, Jamal maneuvered around me to crouch by Porter's head. He checked Porter's pulse and shook his head. "It's weak, but still there."

"What does that mean?" I asked.

"He could have a bigger injury inside or somewhere we can't see," Jamal answered seriously. "If I had a flashlight…"

I pulled West's flashlight from my back pocket. It was still on. Jamal blinked at me as if seeing me for the first time. "You are small enough."

I frowned at him, not understanding.

Taking the flashlight, Jamal checked Porter's eyes for a proper reaction to the light. "You were in the mine." He said it without looking at me. "That's how you got banged up."

It wasn't a question, so I didn't answer him.

"Porter is always chasing us away from the clearing, so we knew something was up." Jamal handed the light back to me and continued talking as he assessed Porter's injuries. "We didn't find it until we were too big to get down the shaft. Jake would have fit a year ago, but it would have been tight, and he's afraid of little spaces. What's it like down there?" He glanced up at me when I didn't answer. His dark eyes amused. "I already know you were down there. That orange dirt on you only comes from inside the underground canyons. Everyone knows that. There are other tourist canyons in the Weatherbee Mine, but there would be no reason to get all scraped up in that one, the wide tunnels are practically paved." He paused, "So what's it like?"

"I'm not really sure." I had not exactly gotten to explore while I was inside.

It was his turn to frown. "But you were down there." His hands were working carefully across Porter's chest.

"I didn't stay to look. I knew he needed my help."

Jamal stopped and stared. "You climbed back up?" He reached over and grasped my arm above my wrist. Turning it, he looked at the long jagged line of dried blood on my upper arm. "You climbed it with that?"

Embarrassed, I pulled my arm away. "He needed my help," I repeated. My uninjured hand automatically moved to protect my hurt arm.

Shaking his head, Jamal went back to his examination. "I don't know who you are, but you are one special kid."

Porter groaned softly.

"Porter? Can you hear me?" Jamal leaned forward eagerly. "It's Jamal. We are getting help." To me he added, "Try not to let his head move. If his neck is injured, any movement could make it worse."

"Okay." I knew that already, but I was fine with Jamal giving me directions. I was suddenly very tired as if a heavy blanket had been draped over me and was weighing me down.

# Chapter 14

Jamal moved around the boulder that had stopped Porter from going further down the steep incline. Kneeling beside Porter, he gently grasped his hand. "Porter? Don't try to move. Can you open your eyes for me? You need to try to stay awake."

Jake bounded into view a few feet away. In his hand he held the red medical kit and on his back was an army green sling backpack. He picked his way through the rocks to us and took in the situation. "You okay?" he asked, looking across at me with a concerned expression.

"I'm fine," Jamal answered before I could.

I smiled at Jake and tried to thank him with my eyes as I had thanked Porter at meals. He seemed to understand.

"How is Porter?" he asked, opening the kit on the ground beside Jamal.

"It was strange, Jake, almost like he was trying to wake up but couldn't." Pulling a few sealed gauze packets out of the medical kit, he handed them to Jake. Tape these over that head wound with…" His hand floated over the kit coming to rest on the medical tape. "This might work. But don't move his head around."

"The cut is in his hair," Jake protested. "How's tape going to help?"

"Those need to be changed for something more sanitary," Jamal pointed out. "I don't really care how you do it as long as there's pressure and no movement."

Jake took a pair of disposable gloves from the kit, pulling them on as he moved over to where I sat. Crouching beside me, he opened the gauze packs one at a time, carefully stacking them to keep them from getting dirty. Jamal unzipped Porter's Jacket.

Porter's shirt was a deep blue. My mind leapt at the simple fact. It seemed comforting for something to be common and normal. His shirt was blue except for a dark patch near his ribs. Jamal peeled his shirt back to reveal the cause. "We are going to need more gauze. This one is deep. He has lost a lot of blood. I hope Rob hurries."

"There's some in my pack." Jake didn't look up from his project, but his expression changed slightly.

"Wait, you carry medical supplies in here?" Jamal unzipped the pack and laughed. "You traitor. Always roasting Rob for bringing the kit his mother sends along, and all this time you have been bringing your own kit? That's cold, man."

I glanced at Jake and caught a slight victorious smile.

Jamal opened the bag the rest of the way, exclaiming over the contents as he pulled out a thick gauze pad sealed in plastic. "You got more gear than my dad carries!" Once the pad was open, Jamal placed it over Porter's wound, pressing lightly as he taped it in into place.

Porter groaned again. He tensed as if trying to move, and relaxed again.

"See what I mean?" Jamal looked over at Jake. "It's like he's trying to wake up, but can't."

"He can't because he was tranquilized." I was getting used to their open mouth stares. Removing the folded pieces of my sleeves from Porter's head wound, I took the gauze from Jake's hand and carefully pressed it into place.

Jake found his tongue first, "What?" He shook his head. "What did you say?"

"West tranquilized him." I could feel the anger rising inside me. West walking free while Porter lay here possibly dying. "West was planning on killing Porter like he did my dad."

"Whoa now," Jamal cut in, adding the last piece of tape to seal the bandage. "Your dad?"

"West put him on a four wheeler and made it look like an accident. Only it wasn't. And Porter knew it."

"I'm out," Jamal announced. "This is way too much for my little brain to compute."

Jake just blinked at me.

"Why did West dump him here instead of using the four wheeler?" Jamal asked. "You used a four wheeler to get to the shaft, didn't you?" He looked at Jake and jerked his head my way. "This kid you called crazy was down the mine shaft and just climbed on out again to help Porter."

Jake's gloved hand went into his sandy blond hair as if he were afraid his head would explode.

"My name is Polly, not Kid," I told Jamal. "West couldn't use the four wheeler. I had the key at the bottom of the shaft. Only he thought Porter threw it into the brush."

"Whaaat!" Jamal was laughing now. "This is better than a movie! Is this a movie?" he started looking around as if expecting to see a crew with hidden cameras.

"It's not a movie." Jake sat on a rock and looked at me. "You are Mason Hamilton's daughter."

A commotion above us sent chills of fear through me.

Jamal laid a hand on my shoulder as he rose. "Don't worry, Polly. It's our people."

Four paramedics in full uniform flowed over the top of the ridge making their way down to us. Two carried duffle bags with their EMT insignia on the side slung across their chests, one carried a back board, and the last one brought up the rear with a shoulder bag with water bottles which he handed out to us as soon as he reached us. We stepped out of their way with the exception of Jamal who quickly filled them in on his findings. Jamal's dad, the EMT with the back board, proudly clapped his son on the shoulder.

"All you need is a couple of years, and you will get to wear one of these cool uniforms, too."

Jamal grinned, and I could see he was pleased by his Dad's public praise.

I sat down, feeling shaky again. I would need to get back into the mine before too many questions were asked. If they took me away from here, I would get thrown back into the rotating housing with my mom or into foster care for good. I needed to find out what was in the mine. I needed to find out what my dad had found. More importantly, I needed my dad's journal.

"You good?" Jake asked, sitting a few rocks away.

"I think I need to step away and clear my head," I answered getting wearily to my feet. I was vaguely aware of the sound of a dirt bike somewhere far below but didn't bother to look around. I didn't even have the energy to open the water I was given. I must have left it on the ground because Jake brought it to me, opened, part way up the incline. Jamal was not far behind.

Thanking him, I took a sip. The next thing I knew, I was seated on the rocks again.

"You good?" Jake asked again, he was holding my un-injured arm to keep me from tipping off of my seat. Jamal was crouched on the other side with a hand on my shoulder.

I righted myself and nodded. "Sorry."

"You don't need to apologize," Jamal handed me the water bottle again. I must have dropped it because now it was only half full. "Don't take it personally, but you are just a kid, named Polly, I know." He put up his hands in mock surrender.

I managed a weak smile, and he grew serious again.

"You have been through a lot today, Polly. Give yourself some grace."

I put my head down on my knees and could hear them whispering over me.

"Look, Polly, since Medical Jake has all these extra supplies, would you mind if I wrapped up your arm?" I heard the bag unzip. "It's not bad, but he's got some peroxide to clean it up and ointment to keep it from getting infected. Is that okay with you?"

I nodded without lifting my head.

"It might sting a little," Jamal cautioned.

I put my arm out, and he set to work.

"I have to go back down today, as soon as you finish," I told them without moving. It was nice to close my eyes to the crazy world around me. I felt Jamal's hands slow, and could tell they were silently communicating over me again.

"Why, exactly, do you have to go down today?" Jake finally asked.

I sat up and looked over at Jake. "My dad got killed because of what he knew about this mine. I found my dad's journal, and I need to know what he knew." I dropped my eyes. "I need to know if he wanted to leave us."

"But couldn't it wait a week or two. Surely girls don't gain weight that fast."

"Really?" Jamal asked, shaking his head in disbelief as he wrapped up my arm. "That's all you have to offer. A weight loss program?"

"I mean, she will still be small enough next week," Jake amended.

I heard someone approaching from the downhill side and watched to see the third member of their band come over the ridge. Robert was shorter than the other two guys. His hair was dark like Jamal's but well cut and very straight. There was an air of confidence in the way he carried himself that the other two teens did not have. I waited as they quickly filled Robert in.

"So, Polly," Jake had not lost his place in the conversation. "Why do you have to go down the shaft today?"

"My dad was murdered and my mom doesn't want me, so I'm about to be tossed into foster care. That is, if West doesn't knock me off first. There's my whole sob story in a nutshell." I met their stares boldly. "This is my only chance."

They looked at each other.

Robert who hadn't said anything up to this point, spoke up. "She's right. She's got a right to know what her dad found. We are going to have to hurry. I could see the medical team from up there. They have Porter on the backboard. They will carry him up as soon as they have him strapped in and stabilized. After that, they will be over here asking her a pile of questions."

"You are going to put her down that hole?" Jake asked incredulously. "It's super dangerous down there."

Robert started walking up through the rocks, and I followed him closely. He was my only chance.

"I did my time in foster care," Robert confided, ignoring the protests of his friends behind us. "You can get through it, but you are right. This may be your only chance, so you need to do this first. You are already pretty banged up which means you will be starting with a handicap of sorts. You sure you want to do this?"

"I am."

He stopped and looked hard at me. "Promise me that you will be careful." There was something deeper about Robert. I could tell he had walked through hard things and come out stronger.

"I'll be careful," I told him gratefully.

We fell silent, navigating the brush at the top of the ridge.

"Maybe rest a little before you set out exploring," Robert

suggested, heading toward the mine. "It will be a few days before they know for sure either way about Porter. Don't rush it."

"He would have died if you hadn't found him when you did." Jamal came up to walk through the tall grass beside us.

Jake sprinted up to join our group. "He's right, Polly. If you weren't so good at chucking dirt clods, none of us would be here."

It felt good to laugh.

"We will watch out for Porter." Jamal was serious again. "Sure, we like to mess with him by coming around the mine shaft now and then, but he's a good guy." As he walked, Jamal bent to break off a long piece of grass, "What I'm trying to say is that we owe you one for saving him."

"Then I'm going to ask for that favor now." I stopped by the mine shaft and looked up at the three friends. "I need you to lower me down in the bucket before the grownups notice."

They exchanged worried looks.

"And don't let West near Porter. No matter what he says. Porter is an eye witness, and you have to protect him, or West will go on to kill more and more people just like he did my dad."

Jamal and Robert nodded. Jake just looked more concerned.

"I can try to climb down, but I am really tired," I confided. I looked at each guy and could tell they were each silently weighing the pros and cons of helping me. "I don't know if I can make it down on my own." I paused, looking at the entrance to the Forgotten Mine. "Either way, I have to go down that shaft."

It was Robert who stooped and pulled the cover from the shaft opening. Jamal stepped in and started pulling up the bucket by the rope.

They must have seen it done before because Jake took the rope and wrapped it around the metal hook Porter had used. I noticed that he was keeping his distance from the hole. He looked back often to check to see if the coast was clear.

"What's this little string?" Jamal asked when the bucket surfaced.

"Porter hung the rope so that I could pull the bucket back down once he was gone," I answered stepping into the bucket and feeling the familiar tightness around my feet.

"You still have the flashlight?" Jamal nodded when I pulled it from my pocket.

It was hard to meet their eyes now. I did not want them to see how nervous I was about going back into the mine. "Thanks for understanding."

They smiled grimly and started lowering me down. I raised my arms to get through the tight spot and watched the circle of fading afternoon light move farther and farther away.

Porter was safe. It was time for my next adventure to begin.

# Chapter 15

I sat with my knees pulled up against my chest and waited silently, making no response to anything they called down. It was rude, but there was no other option. When the paramedics discovered the boys had put me down the mine, there had been a lot of noise up on the surface that I had no trouble making out.

Jamal's dad and another man had called down to me for several minutes, commanding, begging, and even trying to bribe me to get back into the bucket and let them bring me back up to the surface. I had asked them to take care of Porter, shouted up my thanks, and moved away from the shaft and out of the probing beam of their powerful flashlight. Porter needed attention, and they did not have time to waste trying to convince me. After a few minutes, they gave up, turned off the light, and slid the cover over the mouth of the shaft for safety. Now I was alone.

Looking around the wide passage once more, I faced the darkness. "I'm going to make it out of here." My words echoed in the stillness. "And I'm going to take that treasure you are hiding. I'm going to take it and use it to make the world a better place for kids like me. Someone does care. Even if no people do, God cares. I'll help them see that He does."

Even though I was alone, my speech had given me hope and purpose. I knew there were a few people up there who did care. Clicking on my little light, I located my makeshift supply shelf and made my way to that side of the canyon wall.

Climbing up to the ledge where I had stashed my backpack had seemed easy before. Now, my sore muscles protested every foot of the short climb. Shouldering the pack, I moved carefully back down. Robert was right. I would need to rest before I went on.

There was something I had to do first. Removing the transmitter West had given me, I placed it on a high shelf where water could not reach it. I wasn't worried about it getting damaged, but I didn't want it floating out in a flash flood and leading West to a way into the mine. Once that was taken care of, I pulled my jacket from my pack and slipped into it, grateful for its warmth. It seemed the cold of the cave had soaked into me while I sat and waited for them to leave. It struck me as interesting how much of a difference long sleeves made against the chill damp air of the caverns.

Sighing, I looked around for a smooth place to rest. Around the shaft, the ground was littered with little stones and grass bits that came down as we moved around the opening above.

My light caught the dull gleam of the bucket. I had thought, in the darkness, that I had heard them pull it up, but here it was, swinging gently. As silly as it was, seeing the bucket was like seeing an old friend. I noticed something dark hanging over the edge, and I went over to investigate. Amazed, I pulled out two thin warm blankets, a little medical kit, and some energy snacks. I kind of lost it seeing all those things. It was lame to cry, but it meant a lot that they took the time to send them down. Everything from the day came rushing over me. The encounter with West, the unknown about Porter, the strain of the climb, the fear that I could not get the bikers to stop, everything hit me at once. Hugging the blankets, I sat down, switched off my flashlight, and had a good cry. I must have fallen asleep because I woke up feeling cold and stiff. Underground, in the dark, there is no way to tell time so I would have no way to track how long I had been in the mine. Going back to the bucket, I retrieved the other items.

The blankets did not fit in my backpack, but it did not take me long to make a sort of tunic out of one and a wide belt with the other. After eating one, I put the rest of the energy bars into my bag and used some of the leftover string to tie the medical kit to one of the loops on the outside of the bag. Grinning, I imagined what I must look like, draped in blankets and weighed down with all the extra gear. I felt like a regular hobo.

"Hidden treasure, here I come," I called as if I had just finished counting for a game of hide and seek.

Brimming with renewed purpose, I snatched up my dad's journal from where I had laid it on a rock. One of the pictures that was with the journal in Grandfather's desk fluttered down to the stone floor. I picked it up and shone the light on it. It was the shot of the curving canyon wall with that strange white smudge on it. The one I had seen in the book about the mine. I flipped it around and studied it. The smudge seemed familiar somehow. Smiling, I slipped the picture into my back pocket, wondering how long it takes a person to go crazy.

Moving my flashlight beam around, I examined my situation. To my right, the canyon stopped after a few feet. I could see the wall was continuous. Its orange hues were beautiful in the narrow flashlight beam. I turned to face the passageway. My light was swallowed up before it could find the end of the natural tunnel. I moved forward, playing my light over the walls as I went. After several minutes, the passage divided into two. I took off my backpack and fished out my own flashlight. I clicked it on, stashing the small one from West in my bag. The beam was broader and I could see my options better.

Something pale caught my eye. A smudge like the one in the picture was by the right hand passage! I pulled out the picture and almost laughed aloud. I had found it!

Shouldering my bag, I hurried forward to examine it. As soon as my fingers touched it, I knew what it was. Mortar. The grainy substance used to hold bricks in place. I smiled as I thought of the many times I had sat running my fingers through my dad's wet mortar while he quickly and carefully assembled brick structures. Even though he was technically a handyman without an official business to back him, Mason Hamilton was an expert in his trade. Everyone said so. And he had used the tools of his trade to mark the mysterious canyons. An arrow and a symbol had been drawn into the mortar with a thin object before it had dried. This was what Porter had meant when he said to watch the walls.

Sitting down excitedly on the cold floor, I opened the journal. It fell open to a page covered with symbols. Grandfather had apparently spent enough time studying it to crease the book open at this place. Or maybe my dad had. I ran my fingers over Dad's tight, precise handwriting. I missed him more than I could ever express. Yet here I was, holding a book written by him. A book that would guide me on my journey deep within the earth.

———

My finger stopped on the fourth row of symbols, and I moved my light to see the one on the wall. They matched! Sliding my finger down the line I read the writing beside the symbol. "Use this tunnel."

I groaned. I should have been able to figure that out on my own.

I went to the wall and put my hand on the mortar again. In the corner, very small and neat, were the letters MH. My dad's trademark.

Once, when my mom had left without saying when she would be back, Dad had taken me with him to finish up a set of brick steps in a rich neighborhood. At the end of the job, I remembered crouching beside him and watching him carefully carve the letters into the drying mortar. When I asked him why he did it, he had looked over at me and said, "I do my very best when I do a job because I do it for God. I want people to be able to trust my work."

I turned away, hating the fact that my dad had been killed because of a treasure. "Why didn't you give them the secret, Dad?" I said softly. "I would trade a thousand treasures for one more day with you."

Having never been what kids called a 'cry baby,' the recent random floods of tears were unnatural for me. Squaring my shoulders, I headed down the marked passageway, moving the beam of the flashlight over the walls and floor as I went. There was nothing I could do to bring my dad back. I would find the secret entrance and tell the police what West had done. They would know already because I had told Jake, Jamal, and Robert. They would probably need an eye witness, especially if Porter did not…I stopped myself. Porter would make it. Jamal had said that I had found him in time. I chose another train of thought to follow. My dad had taught me to do that when my mind started making up "what if…" scenarios. There was no use getting bent out of shape over something that had not actually happened and probably wouldn't happen.

What about the treasure? If I had the treasure, my mom would want to take me back. I might even have hundreds of families trying to adopt me for my money. It happened a lot in books and movies. That's not what I wanted. I would need to think out a plan where an eleven-year-old, like me, could come out on top without being lost in foster care.

A sound broke its way through my thoughts, and I paused to listen. It sounded like a steady, hollow clicking echoing up ahead. Walking on toward the sound, I followed the curving passage. Another swatch of mortar caught my eye. I hurried over, matching the symbol to the one in my dad's journal.

'Keep right. Hard climb ahead' was written beside the symbol.

Moving forward hesitantly, I rounded the bend. Ahead was a wide cavern. The orange and pale tan coloration rippled through the rock layers as if the walls had been made of layered orange Jello and whip cream. The ground sloped down to a gray-green pool of water. Water dripped from somewhere above, breaking the stillness with its steady plopping.

A wide path ran to the left around the pool. Without thinking, I followed the path, admiring the patterns the drips had made in the silt at the bottom of the water. My foot struck something, and I tripped, catching myself with my hands. Exclaiming at the sudden pain, I scrambled to my knees, cradling my sore hands. My flashlight skittered ahead and disappeared. I saw the beam arch across the high ceiling before it crashed against something below and went out.

For several minutes the only sound in the great echoing cavern was the never changing drip into the pool. Gingerly, I felt around myself. My skinned hands burned, but they were no longer important. Satisfied that I had a decent amount of solid ground on all sides, I squirmed out of my backpack without letting go of it. Feeling around inside, I located the little flashlight I had gotten from West. I thought it strange that something from someone so evil would end up saving my life.

Clicking it on, I assessed the situation. Ahead of me, the natural path I had been following dropped into a black abyss. The weaker beam of this light could reach just far enough to glint dimly off of the scattered pieces of the smashed flashlight below. Moving away from the edge, I looked for what had tripped me. There, across the path, was a small raised ridge of mortar. One last warning before the drop off. I remembered how I had instantly grumbled inside about that tripping hazard and was ashamed for taking my dad's warning so lightly. Retracing my steps, I saw a rough rocky path that led up through a steep mound of rocks. Someone had blasted here, leaving a ragged hole and a pile of rocks that looked like they had been poured out from one of those plastic dump trucks the other kids always seemed to have at the playground.

I started up the narrow path, threading my way carefully through the boulders. I wondered how my dad had carried the mortar he was marking the trail with. How did he get all that mortar down into the mine without anyone discovering the entrance? I knew the answer as soon as I thought the question. Porter had to have been the one to lower it to him down the shaft. I wondered how Porter was doing. Had he woken up? Had he told them what West had done?

"I'm not going to think about it," I told the cavern, pausing for one last look before I slipped around a big rock to stand before the ragged hole into the next cavern. I listened to the steady plopping and was grateful to have something, even something so small, which was consistent and dependable. For all I knew, it had been dripping for years and would go on for years after I was gone.

Checking the hole with my light, I found a solid shelf of rock on the other side. It was smooth and inviting after the rough trail. I would have to be more careful with my light because the narrow beam might not pick up the next marker from my dad. Moving it methodically up and down along the wall, I found what I was looking for. Just before the makeshift rock doorstep into the next chamber, I saw the familiar smear of pale mortar. As I knelt to examine the symbol, my bruised knees reminded me of my close call by the pool. Spreading out the journal, I located the symbol and its meaning.

"Keep climbing," I read aloud. Discouraged, I looked up to the right where the arrow pointed. It was a steep climb, and the rocks looked even more uninviting than the ones I had just gone through. Wouldn't it be easier to go through the opening and find my way from there?

I looked down at my flashlight and knew the answer. I had more batteries, but I did not have another light. I could not afford to have it smashed because I was not willing to walk a harder path. I stared upward, thinking of my dad. He would have had to discover the path and then go back through the hard ways to mark it. It seemed odd for him to have spent so much time marking the mine if he already knew the way. Was dad planning on opening it up someday as a tourist attraction to the public? It would be a good way to get money, but the mine was part of the Weatherbee Retreat. That meant it belonged to Grandfather. My light picked up a smaller bit of mortar further up the trail with an upward arrow confirming my path. With a sigh, I slid my bag from my back and turned to sit with my back against the edge of the arched rock doorway.

In front of me was the rugged trail. To my left was the smooth connecting passage. Beef jerky and water would be my lunch today. Or my dinner. I was not sure what time it was. If I went by my feelings, I had been walking forever, and it was already well into the next day, but my head told me it had only been a few hours. I rubbed my sore arm. Not knowing how long I would be underground meant that I needed to be very careful about how much of my supplies I used. I bit off a piece of beef jerky and flipped to a page near the front of Dad's journal.

"I feel like I have failed my sweet Polly. The divorce lawyer said I would be able to spend time with Polly during the summers, but Gina moves around so much, and it is almost impossible for me to keep track of where they are. I wish I had been a better dad. There must have been something I could have done to keep us together."

My eyes wandered from the page. I remembered the summer that my mom had told me that Dad did not want me to come stay with him. I had cried myself to sleep almost every night that summer. How badly it hurt to be rejected by someone I loved so dearly. Here, in his journal, I discovered the truth. I was not sure which hurt worse, thinking he did not want me, or knowing my mom had lied about something so important.

I read on, "Someone sent me a possible address where they might be so I will write another letter tomorrow morning before I go to the mine. The other letters are here with me, each sent back unopened. I hope someday to show them to Polly. Maybe it is not too late to convince her that I love her and that I did not forget her."

I had to stop and clear my eyes. Clicking off my light, I let the darkness settle around me. "I didn't believe her, Dad," I whispered in the stillness. "I never stopped loving you."

Curling up against the cold stone wall, I laid my head wearily on my backpack and slept.

# Chapter 16

I woke with a start. My hand closed around the flashlight flooding my whole body with relief. I clicked it on, the light seemed almost blinding in the thick darkness. Blinking to help my eyes adjust, I picked up the fallen beef jerky and dusted it off on my shirt. Normally, I went with the five second rule for stuff on the ground, but I didn't want to be starving to death later on and know I had left food behind. I got a quick drink, shoving my water bottle securely into my backpack before shouldering it once more.

Up the steep trail I went, wondering how close I was to the surface. Once I had left the shaft, the ground had sloped down gradually for some time. With all the climbing I was doing, I was sure I had to be near the surface, perhaps I was almost to the secret entrance.

The thought gave me a boost of energy, and I clambered up the rocks, keeping my light moving so that I would not miss the next marker. I was almost to the top when something light-colored on the trail caught my attention. I stopped and looked closer. Laying the journal beside it, I looked over the symbol options. This one was not there. I flipped forward and backward in the book, but there were no other symbols that I could see.

I sat there for several minutes, rechecking the book and squinting and staring to try to make sense of the shape. Could it be the treasure? I scrambled to my feet and looked around with my light. There was no sign of a treasure anywhere. I tried to lift the rock the symbol was on. It turned out to be the top of a boulder that was bigger than me. There was no way I was going to move that. I flipped open the journal again, turning each page individually I scanned them for a line, something that looked like two tiny stacked boxes, and a rectangle of the same height with a tiny dot at the top.

Page after page revealed nothing. I was doing my best not to get pulled into my dad's writing. I would read it all someday, but not now. I only had so many batteries for the flashlight. Something at the bottom of the page caught my eye. It was a line and a rectangle. The markings were the same as the ones in the mortar, except there was no dot in the rectangle shape and the tiny stacked box symbol was not between them. When I turned the page, I understood. It was not a symbol at all. It was a number. Number 180. I had been so focused on finding a strange shape that I had missed the most obvious option.

Turning to page 180, I started to read.

"I found the treasure today. What a day it was! I would love to show Porter, but he still refuses to let me tell him where the entrance is. I don't know how I would do any of this without him. He has been such a good friend to me ever since my first visit to the Weatherbee Retreat Center. I have honored his wishes and kept the entrance a secret. He is afraid that if others know about it, they may hurt me to find the treasure. I hope he is wrong, but have my suspicions.

Enough about that, I have found the treasure! It is much more than I had imagined. I am not an expert, but the coins look like they will be very costly. I am planning on dividing the treasure to keep it from getting into the wrong hands. There is some unrest at the retreat center. Porter says I can do as I see fit with the treasure, but I am to let him know before I take it from the mine. He seemed to think it would be wise not to bring it out until the company clears out. I know who he is referring to. A guest of Mr. Blossom's has arrived, and though his words are friendly, there is something foreboding about him that sets us all on edge. I will assume that if you are reading this, I must be dead. Or at the least, seriously wounded."

I brushed my hair from my face and tilted the page in the beam of the light. The next three lines had been scribbled out making it impossible to read. I could only guess that Dad had written about Mr. West here and it was discovered by Grandfather. Anger welled up inside me. Grandfather knew who had killed my dad. And he knew about Porter. In scribbling out my dad's suspicions, Grandfather was protecting a murderer. My dad's murderer.

Unable to make out the line, I turned my attention to the next legible line.

"I do hope I can explain to Polly before that happens.

As for the treasure, number 180 is the start of the path. The dot is the direction. Stand so the number is upright and Keep the dot ahead of you to follow the trail."

After that, he went on about various methods of transporting the wet mortar. I closed the journal and looked at the 180. Moving around it, so that the number was upright, I crouched down to examine the dot. It was in the top middle of the rectangle. Straight ahead. Looking up, I saw a narrow place between two boulders straight ahead. Stepping over the clue, I walked to the opening. I knew right away that I would have to remove my backpack to fit.

Slipping between the two rocks, I pulled my bag through after me. A little room opened up before me with the same smooth orange and cream walls. Several very small tunnel like passages branched off of the main room. I spotted the mortar. Shouldering my bag, I once again moved to line myself up with the number. The dot was in the top middle of the box, straight ahead again. Only one of the tunnels was directly in front of me. I had to go on hands and knees through it. Even though it was low, there was clearance for my backpack to stay on my back, though it scraped in places. I began to wonder if the path was simply going over and around inside the canyons on different levels. It felt like I had been traveling for miles, but what if I were still directly beneath the mine shaft in a deeper cave?

This passage came out in a long narrow room with three large stone shelves at different levels. I wondered how the dot could help when the only way was up. That is, until I saw that the marker was on the wall. I looked up and over to see only one ledge that seemed to go on past the partial wall of the canyon.

"No use stopping now," I told myself, enjoying the sound of a human voice even if it were my own. I got a drink and pulled out a crumbled biscuit in a baggie. Eating it slowly, I moved forward once more. Three or more turns and a very steep downgrade led me to a little passage in the wall that looked as if it had been chipped away to make it big enough for a man to pass through. I peered in with my light, half expecting to see the gray-green pool. Instead, I found a very small room with a little box sitting against the far wall. It was the treasure!

I had seen enough television at my various placements to know that the room was probably rigged with all kinds of traps. I tossed a rock into the little cave and waited. Nothing. Popping the last bite of the biscuit into my mouth, I stuck my left arm in and waved it around. Of all my body parts, I reasoned that was the one I would miss the least while wandering through the cave. Nothing happened.

"You only live once," I told myself, stepping through the hole. I stood, taking up most of the little room-like crevice. I stepped over to the box and picked it up. Something on the floor caught my attention. It was a folded paper that had been under the box. Setting the box aside, I opened the paper.

On it, horizontally across the center, was a single line of strange characters. Some looked a little like English letters, while at the same time, they were very different from the letters I knew. I flipped it over and found another line of similar letters on the backside. I turned it around several times but could make no sense of the gibberish my dad has so painstakingly put down. Maybe something in the treasure had made him go crazy. It could be that the four wheeler accident had been caused by that instead of West.

I knew it wasn't true. West had made no effort to deny killing my dad when Porter confronted him before I was put down the shaft. Dad was too good with vehicles to be careless enough to go off of a cliff. He had visited the retreat several times in the past to search the Weatherbee Mine property for the treasure he knew existed. I might not have seen him for a while, but I knew that my dad was not impulsive or careless. The paper must mean something.

Carefully folding the paper, I put it between the pages of the journal. Slipping the journal into my backpack, I zipped it up before turning my attention back to the box. Hesitantly, I lifted the lid, still imagining the traps and tricks used in movies. There, gleaming up at me, were five shining gold coins. There were others, five dark coins that I guessed must be tarnished silver.

Was that the treasure? My light flickered, and I grabbed for my bag. I could feel the panic washing over me. Digging through my bag, I located the little pack of batteries Porter had given me. Pulling it out, I put two batteries into my pocket. I slowed my breathing, telling myself I was okay. It seemed as if the darkness outside the little room was pressing in on my light. It was dimmer now than it had been. Changing my mind, I swapped out the batteries for fresh ones, glad they were the right size. If I needed to use up the depleted batteries I could do that later. I clicked the light on and the beam was strong and bright once more. Dropping the used batteries into my bag, I shouldered it, picked up the box, and slipped back out into the main passage. Once again, I changed my mind. I dumped the crumbs from the biscuit bag and transferred two of each of the coins from the box into my bag. This I slipped into my backpack. Once the box was safely back in the room where it had been, I surveyed my surroundings.

I had no intention of giving the treasure to West, but knowing there was more, might be enough to serve as a kind of life insurance. If I was still worth something, Grandfather and Mr. West would be more likely to keep me around.

Flipping open the journal, I moved to the next entry after page 180. My eyes skimmed the page. Dad was excited about the treasure. He had just finished the markers I had followed. He mentioned only once that this was only part of the treasure. I skimmed through the last few pages of the journal. Dad had written about me again. He wrote as if he knew his death was possible, or even probable. Another section was blacked out. I turned to the next page and found a letter Dad had written to me in his clear neat hand. The following page had the words, "In the event of my death, give this journal and all of its contents to my daughter, Polly Hamilton," scrawled across the page. The handwriting was different. It was still my dad's, but the usually clear letters leaned and tilted as if he had scribbled them in a hurry. There was nothing else written in the journal. Nothing about the rest of the treasure.

I was irritated to know that Grandfather was hiding the journal from me even though he had seen the message saying it was to go to me. Maybe that is why they brought me here. They had hoped that I could get the treasure. Well

I had. At least, part of it. The coded paper that was under the box must hold the secret of the other half of the treasure. The part Dad did not want to get into West's hands. What was West up to anyway?

I looked up from the book and turned around slowly, my flashlight inching across the walls and floor in search of the next clue.

There it was! On the far wall was the symbol I had come to recognize as keep right. I checked the floor between myself and the marking. A narrow ravine separated me from the other side. Imagining myself wedged down in it sent shivers through me. Keeping to the right, I moved around the passage to where I could climb up across to the other side. The passage split in two and I stayed right again. Mortar on the floor stopped me only a few feet in.

I checked the symbol with the journal. "Watch your step" was written beside the matching mark. I kept the beam low as I moved forward. I was getting tired, and my flashlight beam sagged even lower. A gaping hole seemed to appear out of nowhere just in front of me. Adrenaline surged through me and the tiredness I had felt before was instantly gone. I would have to be more careful if I wanted to live to see the light of day again. I moved my flashlight beam farther out so that I could see what was coming. Skirting the hole using a narrow ledge path, I pushed onward.

There were several more times that the ground dropped away into a deep canyon below. Once I heard the now familiar dripping, but when I came around the corner, I did not see the pool as I had expected. Instead, there was a steady trickle of water that came from a crack in the ceiling of the tunnel. The water trailed down the wall and dripped down into one of the gaping holes.

"So this is where the pool drip comes from," I mused aloud. "But where does it get into the caverns in the first place?"

My light glinted off of something ahead, and I paused. There, a little ways down the tunnel, somehow attached to the low ceiling, were two very shiny new hinges in the ceiling. Beside this was a neatly built set of three brick steps.

"It is a trap door!" I said with awe. Backtracking, I found a crevice in the wall I had noticed before.

Now I'm not afraid of spiders and such, but I'm also not dumb enough to stick my hand into a black hole in the side of a rock. Using my light, I peered inside. It looked clean and dry.

The crevice was just wide enough for me to squeeze my arm inside. Feeling around, I discovered that it was deep but had a solid back to it. I felt around all of the edges to make sure there was no outlet. Satisfied, I slipped the journal inside. Sitting a safe distance from the pit in the path, I took off my shoe and pulled out the loose sole. Folding the thin paper I had found beneath the box, I slid it under the sole of my shoe and wedged it back into place.

Pulling my shoe on, I looked around. There had to be a quicker way back to the supply shaft. Surely my dad did not go through all those tunnels to get there every time. I saw the mortar on the wall beneath the trap door. It was the same symbol I had encountered on the other end of this passage, "Watch your step". The trail had to be marked going back into the caverns from the secret door.

There was so much more to explore but I could not bear the thought of going back down into the earth. I had no way of knowing how long I had been underground. I had to know about Porter. I had to know that he would be okay.

My only regret was that I would be leaving Dad's journal. I wanted to read it, to know what had happened in his life after he was cut out of mine. More importantly, I wanted to keep Dad's journal away from West and Grandfather. If they got it I was sure I would never see it again. It would have to stay here. Even if I was shipped off to a kid's home, I could always come back, go through the secret entrance and get the journal back. My mind was made up. Climbing up the steps, I crouched beneath the trap door and waited, listening. I could hear the steady drum of water but nothing else. Turning off my flashlight and shoving it deep into my pocket, I took a deep breath. Pushing against the heavy trap door with my hands and the top of my head, I forced it upward ever so slowly. A gust of fresh floral air met me, warm against my face.

# Chapter 17

Though I could not see anything in the blackness, I knew by the fragrance that I was in the garden. How I had traveled so far, I did not know. The water was the fountain which seemed to be crashing just above me. Reaching out my hand, I touched the familiar roughness of evenly laid bricks.

Suddenly I understood. Somehow I was inside the large brick platform under the fountain. My dad had hidden the entrance by building a fountain over it. I could not help laughing softly at the sheer brilliance of it. I thought of Grandfather and West poking around in the woods and the old house never once suspecting that their tourist landmark was also the passage they were looking for.

Allowing the trap door to rest on my shoulders, I pulled out my flashlight, covering the end with my hand as I had done that night in the study. Allowing a thin sliver of light to escape through my fingers, I looked around the little brick room. It was roughly the size of a king sized bed, and only about four feet tall. This would be inside the center of the fountain, with the water in a shallow pool above me and the brick steps that the water ran over, going down on three sides into the narrow U-shaped pool at its base.

To my left, which would have been the flat back of the fountain, was a vertical handle beside a small, horizontal door. Beside the door was a little box with what looked like a rectangle magnet inside.

Pushing up on the trap door, I squeezed my way out, being careful not to hit my head on the low ceiling. It was strange to think that the ceiling in here was the underside of the fountain pool.

There was a pulley system opposite the handle I had seen. Using my legs to keep the trap door from closing, I pulled on the hanging rope. It took almost no effort to raise the heavy trap door. Confident that I could get back in, I scrambled out of the passage and allowed the trap door to close.

Now for the little handle, and to get out without being detected. I could not tell from inside if it was night or day. This was not like my dad. He would not leave something so important up to chance. I looked around. Then I remembered, the fountain had decorative glass gems laid in the bricks! Turning off the light, I waited and was rewarded by a dim gleam of light coming through one gem on each side of the little room. I moved over to the one closest to the door. It was a round gem like the ones on the outside. Only this one was more like the glass tube inside a telescope. I peered through, grinning at Dad's brilliant design. It was curved, expanding the view and giving me a good look at the far side of the fountain. No one was there. I moved to the other side of the low brick room. One gem on each side was a kind of telescope to the outside world. It was dark outside. The light from the waning moon and scattered stars seemed incredibly bright compared to the blackness of the caverns.

I looked around at the dark shapes silhouetted by the moonlight. Nothing moved. Taking the handle by the little horizontal door in both hands I tried to slide it. It moved about an inch and then stuck fast. No matter how hard I pulled, I could not get it to budge. Frustrated, I put my foot against the wall and pulled hard. I had hoped to loosen the door, instead, it opened inward easily, throwing me off balance. It was a working control panel with wires and switches to control the fountain's lights and spray. Now only a thin metal panel stood between me and freedom.

"Dad, you are a genius!" I breathed softly.

Pulling the blankets off, I shoved one of them into the corner of the little room, tying the other around my waist again. If I came back of my own free will, I would not be able to bring supplies with me without raising suspicion. I would pick up the blanket here. If not, I would start at the shaft again and have to remember the symbols. Checking to make sure the coast was still clear, I adjusted my backpack to be ready for the sprint across the lawn. Pushing gingerly against the metal panel, I was disappointed when it did not move. Moving away from the door, I studied it. There was a vertical rubber pad on the metal. The box on the wall caught my attention. Pulling the magnet from inside, I placed it on the door and slid it downward along the rubber pad. The door swung open. Putting the magnet back, I slipped out into the dark night.

Once I was sure I was alone, I pulled the electrical panel closed, sliding it to lock it into place. Next I shut the outer metal door to the panel. There I stood, breathing the fragrant scent of the roses, grateful to be alive. How I wished my dad could have shown me his secret. How I longed to hold his hand and hear him tell about it. Even just to hold his hand and be silent together would be enough.

Knowing I did not have time to stand there wishing, I hurried away from the house up one of the many garden paths I had explored before. I would need to approach the house from another direction or I would give away the secret entrance. Criss-crossing the trails, I circled around to the woods behind the house. There was enough moonlight to help me keep to the grass beside the trail as I dashed along. I had jump roped down this trail and knew it would T with another that led back to the retreat from the back. That would allow me to come in from the direction of the mine and keep Grandfather and West out of the garden. Once I hit the fork in the trail, I turned right, still keeping to the grass for several yards. It is amazing what adrenaline can help you do. My body was exhausted, but I pushed on, knowing the journal would be safe if I played my cards right. A night bird chirped, and I stopped to listen. The woods were quiet as if all of nature was holding its breath to see if my plan would work. I broke a few twigs beside the path and gave a few more broken ones a low toss into the woods. Now I no longer needed to hide my footprints. I trudged along back the way I had come. Back toward the big house. My steps slowed once I was on the path to the kitchen door. I would hide the coins behind the steps before going inside.

Slinking around the hedges, I heard something rustle and dove under the porch. Scrambling further in, I knocked my elbow painfully against the backside of the stairs. I waited, holding my breath. I had made enough noise that if someone was out there, they would know right were to find me. The night sounds droned on and no one came. Letting my breath out in relief, I rubbed my sore elbow silently. Still, no one came. It must have been the wind or an animal passing by.

Getting to my knees, I pulled the plastic bag of coins from my backpack. They glistened in the thin beam of light I allowed through my fingers. I wondered how much they would be worth. In his journal, Dad seemed excited about the value of the treasure. Now to find a good place to hide them. I was considering burying them when I noticed for the first time that one end of one of the bricks stuck out slightly from the rest. That was not like my dad's work at all. Gripping the end of the brick, I pulled. It slid out easily. The middle had been carved out to make a kind of drawer inside the brick. Grinning, I folded the bag of coins and put it inside. That was definitely like my dad. He loved a good mystery which was why he couldn't seem to stay away from the legend of the treasure.

Pushing the brick into place, I found it slid in until it was even with the rest. Curiously, I pushed on it. As if spring loaded, it popped out a little, allowing me to pull it open as I had before. I shook my head in amazement. I must have hit my elbow in my mad scramble to get under the porch. Pushing it into place once more, I shouldered my backpack and moved on hands and knees to where the porch and the hedge met. There I paused, scanning the dark night. It was time to see what I could find out about Porter.

———

"My stars!" Miss Ella exclaimed, her eyes wide with surprise. She stood there looking at me as if I were a ghost.

"Hi Miss Ella, is Porter okay?" I felt awkward standing there on the porch in the dark.

Jane heard me and flew from the stove where I guessed she had been preparing tomorrow's breakfast.

"Porter? We thought he was with you, Polly," she told me breathlessly. "You left together two days ago and, well, we were afraid you had an accident like…" Jane was silenced by a stern look from Miss Ella who had recovered from her shock at my appearance.

"You talk too much, Jane," Miss Ella told her. "If you aren't careful, it will get you into trouble someday. Polly come inside. The bugs are warming up with the weather, and they will be all over my kitchen."

I followed them inside. Miss Ella kept looking at me as if she really did think I had returned from the dead.

Turning to Jane, I returned to the previous subject. "You thought I was in an accident like my dad."

Jane only looked over at Miss Ella who was stirring the

pot that had been left unattended.

"I know about it," I told them. "I know who did it. It was no accident."

Miss Ella left the stove and came over to me, handing the spoon to Jane as she passed her.

"Sit down, Polly." She looked older somehow, and tired as if she had been carrying something heavy and had no place to set it down.

I obeyed and saw her glance nervously at the door to the dining room.

"West is still here?" I asked softly.

She nodded, easing herself into a chair opposite mine at the small kitchen table. "Polly, it is best not to talk about your dad's accident."

"But it isn't right for his murderer…"

Miss Ella held up her hand, her eyes fearful. "Keep quiet." She leaned forward. "Do you want to endanger us all? There's no way to prove it. We have to wait and watch for now."

"You are shielding him then? You knew he killed my dad, and you are still covering for him?" I knew my voice was rising with my anger.

"It's not that simple, Polly. There's no proof to back your accusation. Please, keep your voice down."

"Why? Are you afraid he will come in and kill me? I'm the only one small enough to get down that hole, so he's not going to hurt me," I informed her boldly.

"Interesting point of view."

We all jumped, and I turned in my chair at the sound of West's low voice.

"But you forget, Polly," he went on. "That there are many other unwanted children who can be easily bought."

"Bought?" I repeated. I felt shaky. Had Mr. Blossom actually bought me from my mom? Was that why it was all so quick and my uncle had seemed so awkward about taking me to the retreat?

"You aren't the only one small enough, but you are the most convenient at the time being," West continued. "You somehow managed to get out of the mine. That, in itself, is impressive. The others were not so fortunate."

All of the fear and horror I had felt a moment before at the thought of being sold, were blown away by an explosion of anger inside. I leapt to my feet. "The others? Do you think I don't have a brain at all? You are trying to scare me and it won't work. Got it? I found part of the treasure, but I knew you were greedy, so I left most of it down there. I know there is more, but without the journal, it is impossible to navigate the caverns." I glared at him. "Yeah, I have the journal, too."

He moved toward me, and I backed away quickly.

"I don't have it with me."

He stopped where he was.

I grinned triumphantly. "I guess you underestimated what a 'little kid' can do. You won't get one coin of the treasure until I get Porter back alive," I threatened, banking on Porter being safe with Jamal's father. If West did not know he had been found, Porter would be safe where he was.

"You forget, little girl," West sneered, "that in order to make a bargain like that, you have to have something to trade."

"I have the treasure," I reminded him without flinching.

"You may have the treasure, but sadly, I don't have the thing you want to trade for it." He paused, letting it sink in.

Was Porter dead? Maybe I had not actually found him in time. In such a small town, the news of Porter being injured could have reached the Retreat. Had West managed to kill Porter like he did my dad and once again walk away a free man?

He must have seen me waver, because he laughed. "You thought you were little miss know it all, didn't you? Only you didn't bank on Porter double-crossing you like he did."

This was said for the benefit of Miss Ella and Jane.

"That's not true," I countered quickly, also for their benefit. "Porter didn't double-cross me. You did." If West was sticking to his story that Porter had forced me down the mine shaft, it had to mean that they did not know Porter had been found.

Feeling a swell of relief inside, I reigned in my emotions and squared my shoulders. "You know my terms. If you want the treasure, I'll be around for three days. After that, you can kiss that treasure, and the money you say you spent on me, goodbye."

West's laugh was cold and empty. "We will see what Mr. Blossom has to say about that."

# Chapter 18

I had thought after the fall out in the kitchen that I would have trouble sleeping. After all, according to Miss Ella I had been in the mine only a day and a half, but I was so tired I could hardly climb the stairs with Martha. She waited at the door while I went inside. I could tell that someone had been in there. Even though I left in a hurry two days ago when I was late to breakfast, I knew I had put my things away the night before. Whoever searched it did not have much faith that I would ever return. Clothes hung out of the dresser, and my suitcase was open on the bed.

Pulling some clothes from the drawers, I stood staring at the dresser, unable to think.

"Polly?" Martha came in, putting her arm around me. "Let's move you to another room. You might be more comfortable closer to me."

I nodded wearily.

"You can get a nice warm shower and go right to bed," she was saying as I followed her down the hall to the room beside hers.

I would have been happy to crawl into bed without the shower, but I knew I was filthy from my trek through the mine.

In the new room, there were two bunk beds sticking out parallel from the left wall instead of a queen I had before. I was grateful to be nearer to Martha.

She seemed nervous, much like Miss Ella had been. It

was as if they were afraid my reappearance had brought a new danger to the retreat. "You get your shower, and if you need anything, I'll be right next door." She slipped out into the hall.

"Martha?" I called after her from my doorway.

She turned and looked at me expectantly.

"Do you think Porter is okay?" I needed to know if news of his rescue had made it back to the retreat.

"We haven't seen him since he left with you." She looked as if she might cry. "He didn't have to go with you, Polly, but it was important to Porter that you be kept safe. He said…" She fell silent and quickly wiped her eyes. "You are safe. That's what matters now. You get cleaned up. We can talk later."

I could see she was not going to tell me more. Slipping out of my jacket, I draped it over the arm of the chair.

"Oh, Polly!" she gasped.

I blinked at her dumbly.

She hurried down the hall, leaving me standing in the doorway feeling awkward and confused.

"It must have been awful down there!" She came back with a medical kit. "It is a good thing we have these kits on each floor. You are black and blue, Polly! Look at your arm! I can only assume that bandage used to be white." While she spoke, she helped me to sit in the cushioned chair by the tall dresser.

"I'm okay." I rubbed my sore arm and felt a little nauseous. Maybe I wasn't okay. I leaned forward to look in the mirror and couldn't help staring. The bedraggled child I saw was grimy and bruised to the point that I had trouble telling what was dirt and what was bruises. My hair was coming out of my messy braids in multiple places. My thin face, smeared with dirt, was accented by weary, haunted eyes staring back at me. I looked awful!

"Poor thing, I don't even know where to start." Martha

couldn't seem to decide if she should pull out bandages or try to clean me up. She touched the bandage on my arm and looked into my eyes. "Who did this for you?"

I shrugged.

"Are there people living in the mine?" She searched my eyes as if expecting to find a clue.

"No, I didn't see anyone down there." All I wanted to do was to melt into the floor. "Martha, would you mind if I got a shower before you do your doctoring?"

"Oh, yes, do that. I don't know much about medical things. Porter knew...." She looked embarrassed. Setting aside her medical kit, she looked at me again. "You didn't see him out there?"

I could see she desperately wanted to know if he was okay.

"Miss Ella said it was better not to talk about things like that here," I told her gently.

Martha nodded and said nothing. Her hands worked steadily to remove the bandage from my arm.

I wanted her to know, but if she slipped up, news of Porter's rescue could make it back to West. Porter was an eye-witness and would be able to testify against West. They might even be able to prove he killed my Dad too.

"Oh Polly, that's a nasty cut! You get your shower and knock on my door when you are done and I'll help wrap your arm back up. We will need to put antibiotic on it to keep it from getting infected." She looked me in the eyes. "You met up with someone along the way. There's no way you could have wrapped your bandage so neatly with only one hand." She put up her hand to stop my protest before it began. "There is no need to explain. Go get cleaned up. And try to keep that arm dry."

I smiled and hugged her tightly. "Thank you, Martha."

She looked as if she might cry again and hurried to her room.

———

I sat on the porch looking at the brick stairs as the sun crested the horizon. The light was beautiful and blinding. The door opened behind me, and Jane came out.

"Good morning, Polly," she said cheerily.

"Good morning, Jane." My answer was less cheerful.

"Mr. Blossom is asking for you to join him, and West, at breakfast." She said with a slight curtsey.

I frowned a little. This was not like her. She was too formal. As I got up to follow her, I wondered if West had somehow made them believe that Porter's death had been my fault.

"Jane," I asked as we crossed the entry, "What happened to Porter?"

She glanced at me, but said nothing in reply.

"It has been almost three days since I saw him, Jane. I need to know whatever you know. Time is crucial. Porter could be dying."

"What if he's already dead?" Jane's tone was slightly sour as if she expected me to know more about it than she did.

"Is he?"

"We don't know. He was with you. Now you are here, and he's gone. How did that happen?"

"I don't know. I was in the mine," I reminded her.

"Jane, do you intend to talk out there all morning until my food is too cold to consume?" Grandfather was irritated. I could tell by his tone.

"No, Sir. Here she is." Jane called cheerily as she opened the dining room door and ushered me inside.

"I hope you have a good explanation for your antics, young lady." Grandfather was vigorously buttering his stiff toast. "I expressly told you to stay away from the mine. West told me you must have coaxed Porter to lower you down.

Unless you are going to try to prove that Porter forced you down." His eyes were hard.

"Porter did not force me. West did." I informed him boldly.

"West put you down the mine?" Grandfather asked, glancing at West who was smirking.

"No." They did not let me finish.

"Going into the mine was direct disobedience and must be punished." Grandfather informed me coolly.

Jane had gone to stand in the place Porter had always occupied before, ready for any instructions from Grandfather. It made Porter's absence more obvious to have her standing there trying to look stoic when I could tell she was soaking up every word that was said.

"West is a liar." Taking my seat, I glared at them both.

Grandfather dropped his toast onto his plate and banged down his knife. "Young lady, such rude behavior is not tolerated in my house."

"And his behavior is?" I demanded, gesturing at West.

"West is a guest of mine. Because of this, you will treat him with respect."

"He deserves prison, not respect," I knew I was going too far, but knowing these men were responsible for my dad's death made them repulsive to me.

Grandfather recovered his toast and did not seem to notice it was already buttered as he vigorously applied more. "As it appears you are unable to keep a civil tongue in your head, there will be no breakfast for you. I see no reason to reward such behavior."

"And the treasure?" I decided to follow another tactic.

"You found it?" The eagerness in Grandfather's eyes told me that West had not shared the information about the treasure that I told him last night.

"Yes, I'm willing to trade it for Porter, but I want him alive." I rested my arms on the table between myself and my plate.

Grandfather laughed. "As if you have the right to bargain with my treasure."

The slight look of surprise West gave him told me there was something they both knew about the treasure, but had not said.

"I'm the only one who can get it for you." I watched them closely.

West started to protest, but I could see Grandfather was thinking hard. His bushy eyebrows went down sharply. "You have the journal."

I gave him the sweet innocent look I had often perfected in the mirror. "The journal?" I picked up my fork from beside my plate and toyed with the food I had been forbidden to eat.

"She has it." West blurted. "She said so last night. But it wasn't in her room this morning." West caught himself and fell silent.

"She was in the mine, West, and now she is out." Grandfather looked down the table at me.

"She did not bring up all of the treasure." West grumbled, receiving a sharp angry glance from Grandfather.

"Perhaps, West," Grandfather's tone was polite, yet firm. "It would be wise for you to hold your tongue. If you did not see fit to inform me last night, there is no reason to casually bring it up now in conversation."

West looked unpleasant, but said no more.

Grandfather turned his attention back to me. "You must have the journal. That is how you made it out again. You know of the markings and the secret entrance." He was watching me like a hawk.

"I climbed back up the shaft," I answered truthfully. They did not need to know that I also went back down the same way.

They both gaped at me in silence. Apparently I had enough bruises to back my story. I had purposefully chosen a short sleeve shirt this morning.

Grandfather was the first to recover. "So, you want to bargain for Porter's life." He looked strangely smug. "You will need all of the treasure for a swap like that."

"So you do have Porter?" It was my turn to look smug.

Ignoring my question, Grandfather nodded for Jane to clear his plate. It seemed the conversation had dampened his appetite. "You are going back in that hole today, and you will bring us the treasure." He said firmly. Turning to West he announced, "She goes in the Forgotten Mine shaft today, West. You will take her and put her down that shaft yourself. And don't mess it up this time." When he looked at me, his expression was frightening. "You will get me that treasure, and then we will talk about Porter."

I pushed my food around thoughtfully. Wondering about the paper with the line of characters that I had found with the treasure. Was it a code my dad had invented? If I went down the mine, would I be able to get through the passages without the journal?

"Did you hear me?" Grandfather demanded when I made no response.

"I'm to go in the mine and find you the treasure," I repeated, hoping I was remotely close to the response he was looking for."

He was not pleased. "Now get out," Grandfather ordered.

Blinking at him with a confused look, I did not move. I must have missed something important.

"I told you before that you would have no breakfast because of your rude behavior and I meant it. Go get ready. West will come and get you from the front porch when he is done here. Don't keep him waiting."

Slipping from my seat, I left the room, closing the door behind me.

I walked across the entryway to the stairs. After a few

marching steps on the first stair, I tip-toed back to the dining room door. The sun was streaming through the decorative glass of the front door, giving me a dark shadow which I was careful to keep away from the crack under the door. I stood with my toes at the edge of the hinged side of the door, listening.

"Jane, tell the cook to prepare a traveling lunch for the child." Grandfather's voice carried well through the wide crack under the door. "You may return to your kitchen duties when you have delivered the message."

I heard her retreating footsteps and knew they were alone at the table.

"You botched it with Porter." Grandfather's voice was low. "If you don't get this right, we are both going to be in trouble."

"She knows where the secret entrance is," West protested. "Do you actually think she could climb up that shaft? I saw Porter secure the rope at the top."

"Silence!" Grandfather hissed. "Do you want the whole house to know you were there?"

Their voices dropped too low for me to make out what they were saying.

I was about to head upstairs when I heard West say, "I'll follow her, I can find the entrance."

"Like you followed Mason?" Grandfather's tone was chilling. "West, you have botched it twice. I covered for you before, but the police are asking too many questions about Porter's disappearance. One death can be covered and explained, but a missing person is starting to turn heads. You have to find Porter's body. If he is dead, make his accidental death believable. If not, get him to sign over the rights and get rid of him. He knows too much. Porter's disappearance is drawing too much attention in town."

"It is your staff who are leaking information in town," West's tone was accusing. "They are waiting to pounce on any shred of evidence and go running to the police. You and I both know it."

"They trusted Porter, and he was too smart to slip up." Grandfather's words puzzled me.

They were quiet for a moment, and then Grandfather added, "If a third person goes missing from the Weatherbee Retreat, it will all be over for you."

I could almost hear the threat in West's calculated response. "What are you trying to say?"

"If anything happens to the girl, it will be very uncomfortable for you."

I leaned closer to the door to hear as Grandfather lowered his voice.

"I took a risk taking in this child, West. You advised it, and I went along against my better judgment. I'm telling you now that if there is a third death, you will face it alone. I won't cover for you again. I need that treasure, and if you aren't able to get it for me, I'll find someone who can."

"I'm afraid, Mr. Blossom, that I know too much for you to set me aside so easily." West's voice was hard.

"You are not my only resource, West." Grandfather's tone was equally foreboding. "When I bought the Retreat, I knew about the treasure. For years I have kept this place going, I have played the perfect host to a myriad of guests, I have hired man after man to bring the treasure up from inside the caverns. When Mason discovered the shaft to the Forgotten Mine, I was so close to having the treasure. Then you had to get pushy and blow the whole set up by roughing up Mason and killing him to cover your tracks. I have spent my life keeping this place running. I don't care who holds the rights to the Forgotten Mine. The treasure belongs to me, and there is no one who will stand in my way. Not even you, West. I will get that treasure. When I have it, I will buy back the mortgage for the Weatherbee Mine Retreat Center and live the rest of my days in the comfort I deserve. Either you start showing me results, or I'll permanently cancel our agreement."

A silence followed that sent a chill up my spine. I could imagine them, killers, glaring at each other, sizing each other up.

I tiptoed back to the stairs and hurried up to my room.

# Chapter 19

A soft knock at my door drew my attention. I knew right away it was not Grandfather or West. "Come in?"

Martha appeared. She looked as if she had been crying. "I heard they are putting you back down the mine."

"Yes." I finished tying my shoe.

Martha held out my jacket. "I washed it last night. I thought you might need it."

"Thank you," I hugged her before taking it.

She looked at me, teary-eyed. "I don't know how to help you."

"It is okay," I told her, working my bandaged arm into the sleeve. "Don't worry about me. I can take care of myself."

"I used to think that too."

I paused to look at her.

"Polly, when other people let us down, it is easy to pretend we don't need them." She reached out and smoothed my hair which made me step away without thinking.

"Do you mind if I braid your hair for you before you go?"

I was coming up with an excuse when she got a mischievous twinkle in her eye and added, "Your hair is so wild that it looks a little too much like mine, and it makes me jealous."

I laughed and retrieved my backup brush from the night stand. Running it through my hair, I made my way back across the room to where Martha was waiting. I could not remember the last time I had let someone do my hair. Then, with sudden clarity, I could. I remembered my dad's strong gentle hands drawing my hair back from my damp cheeks. I had been crying, hurt by something kids at school had said. His touch was soothing, and his voice was kind.

"Polly?"

I realized I had stopped, frozen where I was, savoring the memory.

"You okay?" Martha seemed concerned. "I don't have to do your hair if you would rather not."

"What made you think you needed people again?" I asked to change the subject. Some memories were more precious when they were not shared with others.

Martha looked as if she understood what I was doing, but did not protest the sudden topic change. I sat in the chair she pulled out from the desk. Her fingers moved up under my hair, lifting it together away from my shoulders and neck. As she divided it, I glanced at her refection in the mirror. Her face was sad.

"You don't have to tell me if you would rather not," I told her.

She looked up. Catching my eyes in the mirror, she smiled. "Now that I'm trying to start, I don't know where to begin," she confided. Her fingers were working one side of my hair into a neat French braid. "I'll start with the easy part. You asked what made me think I needed people." She smiled at me again in the mirror. "It wasn't a what. It was a who. I'll let you guess who you think that was."

"Porter?"

"Yes." Her eyes got a faraway look. "Here I was, in a new place at a new job. A self-made success. I had been through a couple of rocky relationships, and now I didn't need any-one." She paused thoughtfully. "Porter wasn't like the other men I had worked with. They were oily, always trying to get attention. But everyone I had depended on had failed me. I wasn't about to let some new, slick guy lead me down a rose lined path."

"But he wasn't like that, was he?"

Martha laughed. "Just between us, when I first met him, I thought he was nosey."

I laughed, trying to imagine quiet Porter being nosey.

"Well, he was!" Martha grinned. "He was always asking me if I needed anything or if everything was going okay. He was very kind. I am embarrassed to say I snubbed him. One time I asked Miss Ella about it. She said that if I had met Porter when he first came to the retreat to search for the treasure, I wouldn't have known him. Apparently, he had not always been kind and good. Miss Ella said it was Jesus who turned Porter around and made a respectable man out of him. I didn't care much for religion and all that. So I kept ignoring him, thinking it was all an act."

"Well, what happened?" I asked when she fell silent again.

Smiling, Martha looked at me in the mirror. "You know Miss Ella. She is kind all the way through. Like a good apple. Sweet and crisp. She and Porter kept inviting me to things and including me. They made me feel like a part of their family. I guess, eventually, their kindness worked its way through my shell and allowed my heart to start to hope again. It was the same later when I met your dad. I didn't know him well, but something about him was refreshing and clean. Miss Ella said that after your dad came, he and Porter became friends almost on sight. They talked shop together, discussing all kinds of topics." Martha looked thoughtful, her hands slowing in their work. "They talked about God a lot. I wasn't big on that. I felt like God had forgotten me or didn't care." She reached over my shoulder, and I handed her one of the hair ties I was holding.

"I started to wonder about what made them different," Martha went on

"They make you feel like part of a family. Like you are important enough to care about," I agreed. "It was like I was a part of the family as soon as I arrived."

"Exactly!" Martha agreed. "I never had friends like that. And I fought it for a while, not believing there were people who really cared about someone they barely knew."

"So when did you let them be your friends?" I asked.

Martha looked sad. "It was almost a month after I came. Your dad disappeared, and I could see Porter was really torn up about it." She paused part of the way down my second braid to wipe away a tear and push back her loose hair. "He needed someone to be there for him. I knew he was hurting, and after all he had done for me, being there to listen was the least I could do. We were never the mushy going out for a date type of friends," she corrected quickly when she saw me smile. "It wasn't ever like that. Porter and Mason were kind without wanting anything at all in return. We were professional co-workers, but after Mason died, there was a new kind of bond between the Weatherbee Mine staff team. We needed each other more." She sighed and shook her head with a laugh. "I guess I didn't have trouble saying it after all, did I?"

I grinned as I held up the second hair tie.

"You believe in God too, don't you, Polly?" she asked, changing the subject.

"Yes I do." It was my turn to look thoughtful. "After my dad got saved, I believed there was a God, because Dad did. After a while, I realized that God was not distant or only my dad's God. All the stuff Dad had told me about Jesus dying for my sins and His taking care of everything for me so that all I had to do was believe made sense. I believed, and I knew Jesus was God. I knew that Jesus had died in my place, paid for my sins, and had opened heaven to me."

I saw her nod in the mirror. "I thought so," Martha tossed

the ends of my braids over my shoulders where I could see them in the mirror. "But you didn't at first. When you first came."

"I still believed," I answered uncertainly, turning to look at her, "but after my dad died, it was different." I frowned, toying with my braid. "Things were really hard. When I came here, I was trying to sort out life. I had a lot of questions I needed to be answered. I needed to know God cared."

"And did He?" Martha asked, sitting on one of the lower bunks.

I nodded. "Over the last week, something changed inside of me. I saw God work and knew God could be trusted. I went from believing God existed, to knowing and trusting Him. After that, no matter what happened or where I was, I belonged, because I belonged to Jesus." I glanced at her, feeling shy. "I am not very good at explaining it."

"Polly you aren't alone," Martha told me softly. "I know you are an incredible young lady, but sometimes even superheroes need help from their sidekicks."

I couldn't help grinning at the thought.

"Porter helped me to understand that a lone person can fall, and there is no one to help them up. But a person with others is much safer." She held out her hand and pulled me to my feet.

"Dad was alone when he was killed," I observed swinging my backpack onto my shoulder. It was knobby and uncomfortable. "At the mine shaft, Porter said West killed him, and West didn't even try to prove he was innocent." I slid my backpack to the floor and unzipped it. West had searched it. I was glad I had hidden the plastic bag of coins in the kitchen stairs. "When West found my dad, he told everyone it was an accident," I continued.

"Polly, West didn't find your dad after the accident. Porter did."

I did not look up from reorganizing my backpack. "I guess I knew that. Having others around is important, but it sure does hurt a lot more when they are taken away."

Martha knelt beside me. "Don't you see, Polly. When we love, we risk being hurt. But if we guard and hoard our love, we become hard and cold like the ones who have hurt us."

"I know." I sighed and zipped my bag closed. "I don't understand why Porter didn't tell the police what really happened. If he had, it wouldn't have happened to him."

"I suppose that there was not enough proof." Martha's voice was barely audible. "The Sheriff came out and investigated the place where your dad crashed. West left soon after. I always assumed there wasn't enough evidence against Him. We still don't have any hard proof that West killed him."

We both paused to listen as Jane's irritated muttering reached us from down the hall. "How should I know where she is? Just because I'm in the house doesn't mean you can shout at me when you don't get what you want."

I scrambled to zip my bag and swung it onto my shoulders. Hurrying into the hall, I ran into Jane.

"There you are!" Jane sputtered with relief. "West has been waiting nearly ten minutes, and he is angrier than a hornet. He's down there yelling at anyone within earshot like it is our fault. Hurry up!" Jane handed me a sack lunch and headed back down the hall. "He thinks he can treat us all like slaves," Jane was muttering to herself again.

I followed, waving discreetly to Martha who had stayed out of sight.

# Chapter 20

"What is the meaning of this?" Grandfather's booming voice echoed up the stairs.

"We want to know where Porter is." I was surprised to hear Jamal's voice below.

"So do I, boys, I have not seen or heard from him in days." Grandfather's tone was concerned, almost caring. He knew West had tried to kill Porter, yet here he was playing innocent quite convincingly.

Jane leaned over and whispered, "Better head back up. I'll fetch you when this blows over. The local kids like to hang around in the woods behind the retreat and cause trouble."

Turning to go back upstairs, I watched as Jane hurried down and around the curve of the stairs to the ground floor. She hadn't actually told me to go back upstairs. It was more of a suggestion. I sat where I was and waited.

"Mr. Blossom, Porter always chases us away from the mine shaft. Yesterday, it was this big guy, and we want to know why." Jamal's voice was firm but not disrespectful.

I could hear Robert and Jake agreeing. Why had they come here? They should know where Porter was.

"You are on private property. You will have to leave," West growled. "The Retreat is not open to the public yet."

"Why? You have another body to dispose of?" Robert asked boldly.

There was a moment of awkward silence before West

protested the accusation and threatened to call the police.

"So you don't know where Porter is, but what about the kid?" Jake asked.

I made a face where I sat. He was still calling me 'the kid' even though he knew my name.

"What kid?" West asked. He was responding faster than Grandfather, and I hoped it would get him into trouble.

"You know what kid." Jake clearly didn't care for West. "The whole town knows you have that girl living here. Your granddaughter or something, right Mr. Blossom?"

Grandfather agreed reluctantly.

"I told you the staff could not be trusted," West hissed.

"Trusted with what?" Jake asked. "If you think Mr. Blossom's staff told everyone about the kid, you're wrong. It was us."

Even though I couldn't see him, I could hear the smile in Jake's voice.

West and Grandfather were silent.

"Word is that she was with Porter when he disappeared," Jamal added, moving the conversation along.

"I will have to talk to the police chief about leaking information on private cases," Grandfather said calmly.

"It is a missing person case," Robert pointed out. "They have to give all the known facts so people will know what to look for."

"The police have been searching the area around the mine. He took her there several days ago, and we have not seen him since. We think he forced her down the mine shaft and skipped town." West's story was almost believable.

I stood. If I showed myself now, I would not be put down the mine. I would need Dad's journal to make it through the mine, and I had left that inside the base of the fountain. I went to the bottom of the stairs and almost ran into Jane again. She was waiting there, listening as I had been. There was not time to go up and around to the other stairway.

"I'm ready to go," I stated loudly, causing Jane to give a little scream of fear.

"What are you doing? You go upstairs this minute," she scolded in a sharp whisper.

"I can't." I was still talking loud enough for the guys at the door to hear. "West will be waiting. You know how upset he gets if he is kept waiting."

Before she could respond, I slipped past her and joined the others in the entryway. West and the guys were on the porch. Grandfather was just inside the entry with his hand on the door as if ready to slam it if needed. He moved over when I came to stand beside him.

"Oh, good, at least you found the kid!" Jake exclaimed when he saw me.

"Yes, she had been put down the mine shaft. It is such a dangerous place down there." West tried to appear relieved. "We heard her yelling and managed to pull her back up. It is a miracle she is alive at all."

"Who put her down?" Jamal did a great job looking surprised. I on the other hand wondered how West thought he would get away with making up stories when I was still around to tell the truth.

"Porter did." West looked at me with his cold dark eyes. "Isn't that right?"

"Yes." It was true. Porter had done it under orders and at the end of a gun barrel, but he had done it.

"See," West cut in before I could say more. "It was a terrible thing for him to do to a little, helpless kid. I didn't know he was capable of such a thing. Don't get greedy boys. It will only lead to harm."

I wanted to laugh scornfully at his hypocritical advice, but held my peace instead.

Jamal casually changed the subject. "Looks like you two are going somewhere. Are you headed into town?"

"Uh," West looked at Grandfather for a cue.

"They have to be," Robert put in. "The sheriff still has people searching for her. They will need to know she's safe."

"As a matter of fact, that is where they were heading," Grandfather agreed. "You know the phones don't work well out here. West will let the police know she's been found. After Polly's traumatic experience, we thought we should give her a day to recover." He turned to me. "Unless you think it would be too much so soon after." He obviously wanted me to say that I would rather stay back.

I smiled sweetly at him. "Going into town sounds refreshing. Having people around will calm my nerves."

He cocked an eyebrow at me, but did not protest. "Have a good time. Don't be long. We will need to start preparations for the opening day."

With a nod, I stepped out onto the porch. I felt safe with the guys around. West could not do anything to me with so many witnesses.

"That's great! We are heading into town too. Mind if we hitch a ride?" Robert asked eagerly. "Jake's bike is running rough, and we need to get a replacement part."

Everything about West's body language said no to Robert's question.

"It would save us a lot of time, and we promise not to be any trouble," Jake added. "You can even let us out at the dirt bike shop on the edge of town, if you don't want to be seen with us."

Grandfather nodded once, and I saw West tense up. He was angry but hid it well. "Alright, but only if you promise to stay away from the Forgotten Mine. It's dangerous."

Robert and Jamal looked at each other and both shook their heads. "We can't do that, Mr. West. If you want us to be quiet, or to ride in the back, that we can do. But we can't promise not to go near the mine. We wouldn't be good citizens if we didn't help look for Porter."

"I'll get the keys," West muttered, starting inside.

"You have them in your hand."

A fierce glare silenced Jake.

"You wait by the car." West's face was hard.

They did not hang around to ask questions. When they were a few feet away, the guys looked back to see if West was watching, and I saw them exchange looks of triumph behind him.

"Go wait by the car," West instructed me in an angry growl.

I slid my backpack off and set it inside the door. I knew Grandfather would look inside it, but I didn't care. There was nothing important in there right now. As I walked toward the guys, I overheard West muttering.

"Taking the girl into town is moronic. People will ask questions."

I stopped, stooping to re-tie my shoe within hearing distance.

"You are the one who lost the body, West." Grandfather's tone sent chills up my spine. "I want people to know she's okay. If these boys are asking about her, so are the others in town. There are enough rumors going around without adding a missing child. Once she is seen in town, people will stop asking where she is and assume she's safe. That will give us time to put her into the mine again. I want that treasure, West."

"But she will talk."

Even though I wasn't looking at them, I could tell their attention was on me. I rose and dusted off my pant leg before heading for the Explorer.

"Polly?" Grandfather called.

I stopped and looked back.

"Don't talk about the mine while you are in town. Or anything that happened with Porter, okay? Let West talk to the police and answer their questions. They need to know you are safe, but reliving the trauma might cause more harm than good in this situation. Will you do that for me?" His tone was almost kind.

"You don't have to worry, Grandfather. I understand." I continued toward the car hoping he would not press for a promise. Somehow I needed to figure out a way to get my Dad's journal without giving away the secret entrance to the forgotten mine.

"Polly, Porter is asking for you," Jake whispered when I joined them.

"He's okay?" I felt shaky with relief.

"He's pretty banged up and had to have a good number of stitches, but Dad said he will make it," Jamal confirmed. "He keeps insisting on talking to you though."

"Do you know what he wants to talk about?" I glanced over at West and Grandfather. I could tell by his body language that West was not making any progress in his arguments.

Jake shrugged, "No idea. Porter won't tell us anything. He keeps saying that he has to talk to you before he goes, and time is short." Jake grinned, "And no, we don't know where he's going. In case you planned on asking."

"The nurse mentioned that Porter had already had guests and could not be bothered when we went to see him yesterday," Robert added. "Jake's sister is interning at the hospital and said the visitors were very official and that no one was allowed in the room while they were there. She said they talked for over an hour. After that he started asking for you."

"You didn't ask him why?" I asked, trying the handle of the Explorer. It was locked.

Jamal shrugged, "We haven't had a chance. Porter was hurt pretty badly, so we weren't allowed to see him more than a few minutes the first time we went."

"When we went this morning he asked us to come find

you," Jake added. "We could tell it was urgent, so we came here right after."

"But do you have a real candy store? Or just one of those lame tourist shops?" I asked tossing my braid over my shoulder.

They looked confused for an instant. Jake glanced up and saw West approaching. "It's pretty sweet. No pun intended," he joined in, bumping Jamal to get him on the same page. "Good prices and a nice selection. You will probably be surprised at the prices in town. Did you bring money?"

"Oh, I didn't think of that!" I also didn't mention that the only money I had was the gold and silver coins hidden behind a loose brick under the kitchen stairs. Why hadn't I checked behind it? If the brick was loose, it was intentional. Was there another clue inside or behind the little brick drawer I had discovered? I wanted more than anything to run look behind that brick. It had been dark before, and I never thought of looking. Now, curiosity was killing me.

The Explorer beeped and flashed as West unlocked it. He got in without speaking, his face dark with anger.

For a moment, I was afraid I would not live to explore this new mystery.

# Chapter 21

"Look, all you have to do is say "I'm running away," and run up that hill. There's a railroad track just over it. You turn right onto the tracks and run until you see a wide yellow ribbon tied around a big oak tree. Take another right onto the little trail that goes by the tree, and it will take you back up over the hill." Robert paused, "Did you get all that?"

"Yeah." I didn't offer to repeat it.

He looked skeptical. "When you come back over the hill, check to make sure no one is watching and don't leave any tracks. There's a gas station there. It's a big fancy one. You won't be able to miss it. Next to that is the bus station." Robert held out his hand and Jake slapped a five dollar bill into it. Handing the bill to me, Robert glanced around. "Go to window 3, even if there is a line, and get you a ticket to the hospital stop…"

"Don't you think that will be suspicious?" I interrupted. "What?"

"My going right to the hospital as soon as I get into town. Everyone will see me at the gas station and bus station. Those are high traffic areas. Haven't you ever watched any spy movies?"

They looked at each other.

"Look, Polly, this is our only chance," Jamal answered. "West is going to come out of the police station any minute. The only reason you aren't in there too is because he's afraid you will tell what really happened. This is our town. You will have to trust us."

I glanced nervously at the police station behind me. We were in a grassy park-like area that sloped upward into a long manmade hill designed to block the sound of the train when it passed by. I thought of my conversation with Martha. Letting my breath out, I nodded. "Okay."

They grinned at each other.

"Here's your disguise." Jamal handed me a beat up grey baseball cap and a small plastic bag. "It's fake teeth." He told me when I held up the bag to examine it. "Don't worry. They are clean."

"I'll take the hat, but the teeth are a little too much." I took the hat from him. Undoing the Velcro, I reconnected it around my belt loop. "The teeth will draw more attention."

"Trust me. You want to wear them. And do an accent if you can."

"Do you need to hear the instructions again?" Robert asked.

"No, I got them." Reluctantly, I shoved the bag into my pocket before starting for the hill.

Robert yelled after me, "You forgot the first one!"

"I'm running away!" I shouted back. That was all I said because the hill was steep and at least six feet high. I paused when I got to the top. Looking down, I saw the guys moving toward the police station. I wouldn't have any extra time to rest. I scrambled down the steep embankment, pausing to check for trains before I got to the bottom. There was a gap of three or four feet between the hill and the tracks that was filled with gravel. If I was careful, I could run along it without turning up the stones and leaving a trail. On the other side of the track, there was a mowed strip that ran along the line, and then tall weeds and woods on a steep downward slope.

Looking around, I spotted a pile of round logs that were

as wide as me but only about a foot long each. I guessed they were from a tree that had been cleared from the track. Wrapping my arms around one on the top of the pile, I grunted as I lifted it. I couldn't have done it if the wood had been fresh. This log was dry and heavy, but manageable. I stumbled over to the edge of the mowed grass. My goal had been to set it down, but I got it to the ground with some help from gravity and managed to miss my feet. Giving the log a shove, I sent it tumbling down the hill into the ravine below the tracks. That would give them a trail to follow and buy me more time, unless I had already wasted the lead the guys had given me. I went back to the tracks.

I knew Robert had told me to run on the train tracks, but that was dangerous. A boy at one of my schools got killed by messing around on an active track. I would run along the gravel and hope for the best. Glancing once more up at the top of the hill, I started to run. Keeping myself to a quick jog so that my shoes would be less likely to leave tracks when I pushed off.

There were trees on the right that seemed to be growing just over the crest of the hill on the town side. Robert had said to run until I reached the big oak with a yellow ribbon. I hadn't bothered to ask him what an oak looked like. I knew what a yellow ribbon was.

My eyes darted from the uneven gravel to the line of trees. I was even with the first of them now and still could not see a ribbon of any color. I slowed a little to catch my breath. There! A grand tree with a wide trunk and thick spread of branches stood in the line of younger trees along the hill. Around its giant trunk was a wide yellow ribbon that had been tied into a bow that was bigger than my head. I stuck to my gravel path until I saw a little foot path at the crest of the hill. The grass was already worn in a trail up to the tree. Sticking to it, I made my way up the hill, sparing a quick glance back the way I had come. When I reached the top, there was a miniature park with a few benches and an old stone drinking fountain. A sign by the tree showed a picture of a soldier hugging a girl by what I assumed was a younger version of the big oak. I didn't stop to read about it though. I guessed people came to see the tree and sat on the benches to watch the train go by. It would be fun to do that sometime when I was not running for my life. I pulled the baseball cap and fake teeth out of my pocket.

I had no desire to wear them, but I had agreed to trust the guys, and that meant following their instructions. I put the hat low over my forehead and maneuvered the fake teeth into my mouth. "Here goes," I muttered, enjoying the garbled lisp the teeth gave me.

Crossing behind the gas station, I cut through on a well-worn foot path to the bus station. The door was heavy, and I leaned in to open it. A man pulled it open from the inside causing me to stumble through.

"So sorry, little girl. Are you alright?" he said in a thick English accent.

"I'm alright. Thank you for askin', Sir," I said, lisping in my best Mississippi accent. I'd lived there for a month and a half, and it was the best accent I could do.

I moved past him confidently before he could ask me anything else. Once I had weaved through the benches, which were mostly empty, I stopped to look for window number three. The numbers had been freshly painted above the booth-like windows, and the white stood out clearly against the deep blue of the wall. I went to the window under the white number 3.

"I need one ticket to the hospital stop," I told the man, letting the brim of my hat hide my face.

"One ticket, for Polly, coming right up."

I looked up at him in shock. He was a middle aged man

with thick, blonde curly hair and a very friendly smile. My first impression was that he was a fun, cheerful person to have around. He looked like he spent more time enjoying the outdoors than he did in the little ticket cubical. I felt safe with him right away.

"My son, Robert, said that they could get you to wear the teeth, but I didn't believe them," He laughed.

Frowning, I considered the new information. The teller looked nothing like Robert. Robert's hair was dark, almost black, and very straight. How could this curly blond man be his dad?

"You can take them out if you want," Robert's dad told me without trying to hide his grin. "I know who you are. Wait right there." He placed a 'be back soon' sign on the narrow counter between us and disappeared into the back. I spit the slobbery row of teeth back into the bag and tossed them into the trash.

A moment later, Robert's dad emerged from a door at the far end of the counters. He came over to me and gestured for me to go first to the side door of the station. I glanced around. Only one man remained in the bus station lobby. He was holding his bag to his chest as if he suspected he would be robbed while pretending to sleep. I didn't see any other option, so I went to the door the man indicated, and he walked along with me, chatting as we went.

"You had us worried, Polly. When I heard they put you back down the hole, I…well, let's just say Robert got an earful about wisdom."

"I needed them to put me down there," I told him. "They did me a big favor and could have saved my life."

The man held the door without responding, studying me as he did so.

I went outside and waited for his next instructions.

"My car is the brown one over there," He said, strolling

toward it. I got the impression that he was instantly friends with everyone he met. "You might not believe it, but that car is actually white. The dust around here coats everything. Once I convinced Robert and his friends to stop drawing on it, I didn't have to wash it anymore." He opened my door as if I were a lady, and I got in.

Once he was situated in the driver's seat, I asked him what I had been wondering since I saw him. "Are you Robert's Dad? You don't look anything like him."

He smiled, "I guess I did forget the introduction part." He started the car and stuck out his hand to me. "I'm Theo Thimbleton."

I shook his hand, "Nice to meet you, Mr. Thimbleton."

He smiled. "You are a polite little Polly, and it is a pleasure to meet you. You can call me Theo. Or Mr. Theo, if that's too casual for you." He kept talking as he craned his neck around to check behind him and backed out of the parking space. "I know it's hard when people want you to call them something, but it feels awkward to say it, you know? Then you go around never saying their name because you don't know how to sort it out inside."

Not sure how to respond, I let the subject settle before going back to my original question. "But you don't look like Robert."

"You are observant too. No wonder the boys got so involved." Theo pulled out onto the street. We had only waited for one car, and I only saw two others driving.

I had asked twice, and Theo had not responded to my question. I figured he didn't want to talk about it. I changed the subject easily. "There are not many cars around. When does tourist season start?"

That turned out to be the jackpot of conversation starters. As he drove, Theo pointed out all the improvements that had been made to prepare for the tourists who would be coming in next week. He told me about the town's economy, how they depended on tourism, and how someone getting killed in a four wheeler accident had hurt the flow of tourists to the Weatherbee Mine. I tried to probe for more information, but he would only say, "It was a messy business, and I don't think it has been properly sorted out yet."

"When did Porter come to work here?" I asked. The town was small, and we were already approaching the three story hospital.

"Oh, he didn't come to work. Not at first. He came with that oily West character who is back at the Weatherbee Mine now. They were partners of some kind. Only Porter seemed to have had a change of heart after that brick layer Hamilton started working around there. Hamilton was a nice guy, friendly and cheerful. The sort that are nice to have around. He didn't come into town often though, they kept him busy out at the retreat." Theo was taking his time picking a parking spot even though there were at least ten open spots across the hospital parking lot. He laughed, "I got sidetracked. Where was I?"

"Porter changed," I offered.

"That's right. You are a good listener, Polly." He smiled at me and apparently settled on a parking spot a few spaces ahead. "So, Porter met the Lord. Changed everything. He was a different man after that. Jesus can change a person if they stop fighting and let Him do it." He pulled in and put the car into park. "Polly, do you believe Jesus is God and that He paid for our sins so we can be forgiven and be right with God?"

"Yes, I do," I answered.

His broad smile appeared. "I'm glad to hear that! You looked like you could use a good solid family, and I just had to know if you had one."

I frowned curiously, and Theo laughed.

"Everyone who believes in Jesus and says yes to His free gift of salvation becomes a part of His family. If you are a part of Jesus' family, and I am too, that makes us related. Can I be your crazy uncle?" Theo asked, watching for my first reaction. "I've always wanted to be a crazy uncle to someone."

I smiled back, feeling happy myself. "Sure, Uncle Theo."

"It's a dream come true!" Theo was genuinely happy. I could tell it was not an act. "Now that we have settled that, let's get on with this secret mission." Theo turned off the car and pushed open his door.

We got out and walked together to the hospital door. Even though we didn't speak, we were both still grinning.

# Chapter 22

When we entered the hospital, Uncle Theo called the lady behind the desk by name and chatted easily with her. She was a sour-faced old lady, but Theo treated her as if she were a dear friend as we signed in at the front desk. She complained about the work load, her aches and pains, and the hassle of the new security protocol as she printed little sticky visitor badges for each of us. Theo talked about the beautiful weather and exciting tourist season that was about to begin. She was determined to be gloomy, so we put on our tags and headed to the elevator.

"Porter was pretty banged up," Theo reminded me seriously as the elevator doors closed. "If it is too much, you don't have to go in."

"I saw him right after it happened." I didn't want Theo to see how nervous I was. At the ravine it was different because Porter was not fully conscious. Until this point, I hadn't thought about anything besides the fact that he wanted to see me.

"Well, if you need to step out at any time, you can give me the secret signal, and I'll cover for you." He gave me an exaggerated wink, and I couldn't help smiling.

The elevator beeped on floor two and stopped. The doors slid open revealing a hall that ran an equal distance in both directions. I hadn't spent much time in hospitals, but even I could see this one was small and dated.

Theo led the way to the room without hesitation. His knock was answered by a man in a grey suitcoat. If the man was trying to blend in, he was doing a very poor job of it.

"Are you with the police?" I was impressed the guys had been able to arrange this level of security.

He smiled stiffly and stepped aside to allow us into the room. "You must be Polly."

"Polly?" Porter's voice came from beyond the curtain across the room. The colors reminded me of re-runs of old movies my grandma watched while I was with her.

Realizing that I was delaying my meeting with Porter, I moved forward. Acting confident sometimes helped, but this time was different.

"Hi, Porter." I stood awkwardly, not knowing how close to get and trying not to stare at the stitches on his forehead or the bandage on his arm. The blanket was up to his chin but he looked strangely bulky beneath it.

"Hi Polly. Thank you for coming." Porter rotated his hand so that it was palm up, and I went over and clasped it in a stationary hand shake.

The police-like man brought a chair close to the bed, and I sat in it facing Porter. He turned his head on the pillow and looked at me.

"I wanted to tell you before they took me," Porter's eyes were serious. "I wanted you to hear it from me."

I could not read his expression. That made me feel uncomfortable inside. I waited. My mind raced through a hundred possibilities for what he was about to say.

"West isn't the only bad guy at the Retreat." Porter's eyes did not leave mine.

Again, I waited.

"I used to be West's partner." He paused to let it sink in.

"Theo told me," I said softly. There had been so many times in my life that I had been told hard things and been expected to roll with it, that I found it easy not to react. I would hold it together and think about it later when I was alone. Porter needed me to hear it all now.

"Do you mind if I tell you again?" Porter's face was earnest, as if telling me was some kind of dying wish. "I want you to know the whole truth, everything I should have told you before." He shifted uncomfortably and waited for my response.

"Theo only told me that you were partners." I didn't know what else to say. "I would like to hear the rest."

I could see the relief in his expression. "Polly, I came to the Weatherbee Retreat to find the treasure. The same treasure your dad wanted to find. He had been there before and was excited about the historic discovery. I didn't care about anyone's history, only my own future. I was there to steal the treasure. West and I convinced Mr. Blossom that we were there to help him get the treasure. We were making good progress with him when West's temper got out of hand. He said stuff he shouldn't have, and Mr. Blossom got suspicious. He did some research and discovered West and I were wanted in several other states for breaking the law and conning people out of their money." Porter's gaze moved up away from me, and I saw his jaw tense as he clenched his teeth to hold back some emotion. He blinked a few times before going on. "That's something I'm so ashamed of now. If I could go back and change it, I would in a heartbeat." He paused, collecting himself. "Your dad's death was never part of the plan. Polly, please believe me. If I could have stopped it, I would have." He was looking at me again, begging me to take a chance and trust him again.

"Just tell me what happened." My voice was strange and tight.

"When Mr. Blossom discovered what we were, instead of turning us in, he forced us into a new agreement to split the treasure two ways. He would get half for keeping quiet, and we would divide the other half. We had no choice. Our last job hadn't ended well, and West and I were on the run from the law. Besides that, we did not have enough cash to start another scam because I had spent the greater portion of it on a personal endeavor. West and I knew that if we left the retreat, Mr. Blossom would send the police after us. The only way out was to agree to his terms and find the treasure. We were there a month or two before your dad came and had made little to no progress actually finding the treasure. Your dad, on the other hand, somehow managed to find the secret entrance almost immediately. You probably know he had been there several times before. That was why your grandfather invited him back. Mr. Blossom suspected your dad had already found the entrance on a previous visit and wanted West and I to follow him to it."

I pulled up my knees and hugged them tightly to my chest without knowing I did so. There were so many people responsible for my dad's death that I didn't even know who to blame. Resting my forehead on my knees I tried to process what I was hearing. How could Porter be one of them? How could my secret friend, the one who stood up for me, also be the one responsible for murdering my dad?

Theo touched my shoulder, and I jumped.

"You alright, Polly?" he asked gently.

I nodded, embarrassed. Though I faced Porter once more, I kept my knees up as if they were a barrier between myself and the world. "You can keep going."

For the first time, I noticed that the officer in the corner was taking notes.

"Are you going to put Porter in prison?" I asked. The officer looked up when no one else responded. Realizing I was talking to him, he glanced at Porter before nodding at me. "He will get a lighter sentence for working with us to help locate and capture West, but he still has to pay for what he has done." The man's tone was mater-of-fact, as if sending people to jail was a normal part of his day.

"Polly, my going to prison is what I deserve." Porter's words were brave but I could tell his emotions did not match his words. He was scared. Like me, his life was changing. Only for him, doing the right thing was going to cost him dearly.

"You will let him get better first, right?" I asked the officer.

"Yes, he will be moved to a secure hospital tomorrow." I don't know if he remembered I was still a kid, or if I looked as much like I was about to cry as I felt, whatever it was, his whole demeanor shifted. He lowered his paper and gave me his full attention. "Don't worry, Polly. Porter will be given a fair trial in court before he serves his sentence."

I scolded myself for caring. And for believing that I had a friend who cared back.

"Polly, a lot is going through your head right now," Porter observed gently. "I want you to know the truth. You can ask me anything."

"Why didn't Grandfather get rid of you?" The question seemed to leap out on its own.

The men glanced at each other, and I could see they did not understand.

"I mean," I tried again, "you knew West was a crook, and Grandfather was basically his partner. Why didn't they kill you like they did my dad? Or at least fire you from the Weatherbee Retreat?"

"They couldn't afford to, Polly." The mischievous twinkle in Porter's eyes reminded me of the night we had decided to be secret friends. "I own the Forgotten Mine. Anything found underground in those caverns would belong to me."

"But how? I mean, why did they let you buy that?" I asked, confused.

"It was a kind of insurance plan I had in case West tried

to cross me. The only way they would get anything was to keep me happy and alive. West and I had a system down for meeting potential customers. I would go in, meet them, build trust, and then West would come and add a little pressure if needed. Following the plan, I called ahead and booked an off-season single room at the retreat. On the first night, I had an uninvited look at the Weatherbee Retreat's financial books. Even I could see Mr. Blossom was in trouble financially. So, I talked it over with his lawyer, James Reyer, who lived out of town. The man was sick of the years of promises and ready to get the Forgotten Mine and its hazardous shaft off of his client's hands before there was a lawsuit." Porter paused for a moment to catch his breath. I could see he was getting tired. "Mr. Reyer was not exactly a model of good character, and it did not take much to sway him to work it out so that I could buy the mine. He flew in, and we had a meeting with Mr. Blossom the day before West was scheduled to arrive. Reyer and I convinced Mr. Blossom to allow me to purchase the mine with the understanding that I was doing it to help the retreat stay afloat. That was what had happened to the money West and I came with." Even though tricking West by buying the mine had happened years ago, Porter still looked smug when he mentioned the money he had so shrewdly invested. "Though I never actually said it," he went on, "Henry Blossom was desperate enough to believe that I would sell the mine back to him once he had his feet under him again. Only his lawyer and I both knew that it would never happen. After West arrived, and before we had fully convinced Mr. Blossom to work with us, your dad showed up and screwed up the whole plan." Porter's grateful smile did not match his statement.

I missed my dad so much and wanted to hear stories about his time at the retreat. "How did he mess it up?" I prompted, toying with the end of one of my braids.

"He was so kind. So good to all the staff. It wasn't a show. It was like he had a secret fountain of kindness that just seemed to flow over anyone who got too close." Porter sighed and closed his eyes for a moment, wincing ever so slightly.

"Do you need us to come back later?" Theo asked sympathetically.

"There is no later," I cut in. "West is at the police station and the 'little girl ran off' story the guys are telling will only last so long. I need to know now."

Porter opened his eyes and smiled over at me. "Yes, you do. I'm sorry. I just needed a second. I'm okay." He took another slow breath before going on. "That was a very long answer to your question, Polly. The short answer is they could not afford to get rid of me while I owned the mine. I gave myself the position as the butler or head servant of the house so I would know if anything shady was going on. They had to agree because they knew I had no plan of selling out to them and losing my part of the treasure. I had everything right where I wanted it. The only problem was that the more I talked to your dad about God, the more I felt the weight of guilt for what I had done and who I had become. Whatever was hidden in the mine stopped being important. Your dad showed me that I needed something so much more valuable than a treasure. I had always been able to get anything I wanted. This was different I knew there was no way I could buy it or even cheat someone out of it. I needed mercy." He closed his eyes and took a slow breath. "Do you have any other questions?" he asked without opening his eyes.

"Why didn't you tell the police that West killed my dad?"

Porter bit his lip, and his face looked pained. It was several minutes before he could answer. "Because I was a coward, Polly," he blurted, blinking back tears. "I am a coward. I knew in exposing West, I would expose myself. I was scared. I knew that a single paper, the rights to the treasure, was the only thing keeping me from being killed, too. Time passed, and that only made it worse. I told myself that I didn't have any real proof. I knew it was West all along, but there was nothing solid to show the police. When it happened, I went looking for your dad. I wanted to do what you did for me, Polly, to find him alive and save him. He would tell the investigators what happened, and West would be canned for good. I prayed so hard that he would be alive when I found him." Porter was silent for a while. "But that time God said no."

We all waited in silence as Porter sorted out his thoughts.

"It was such a heavy weight hanging over me. I lost my best friend, and I was too chicken to do anything about it. The police investigators had asked questions. I hadn't lied, but I knew more than I let on. Then you came, and I saw the hurting little girl Mason had loved so much. I saw how much my silence had hurt you. That first night, when you offered to be secret friends, I thought my heart would break. God started working on me, and I knew I had to come clean. I was still scared of what it would cost. That's why, once I knew you were safe in the mine, I challenged West. I knew he would get angry. He doesn't think straight when he is angry. I don't think he intended to kill your dad, but he lost control and was smart enough to cover his tracks. I had hoped he would kill me." Porter looked up at me. "It was selfish of me. I knew you had your dad's journal and that you could make it out of the mine." He smiled a little. "I saw you take it from Mr. Blossom's study in the wee hours of the morning. You are so much like your dad. Maybe a little too much. I honestly never thought you would be able to climb back up the shaft. So it never crossed my mind that you would be able to do it in time to save me."

"Are you sorry I did?" I hugged my knees tighter.

"No, Polly. I'm so grateful. What you did took a lot of courage. You put yourself in danger for me. Your dad always did what was right, even if it cost him. He didn't share the location of the mine opening because he knew the money would go to hurting other people. He was the reason Mr. Blossom could not follow West's plan to put a child down the shaft. Mason Hamilton was quick to stand up for those in need. You are so like him," Porter repeated fondly. "I wish he could have known what an incredible young lady his Polly has grown up to be."

Wiping my eyes with both hands, I waited for him to go on.

"Polly, you showed me what true courage looks like. I'm ready to stop being a coward and to stand up for the truth. It will cost me, but not as much as it has cost you." He paused before adding, "Can you ever forgive me, Polly?"

I wanted to ask more questions, and to hear more about my dad, but I knew there was not time. Porter was pale and tired. Letting my feet slide to the floor, I sat there for a moment. In that moment, I realized I had already forgiven him. He had been a friend to my dad, and had been hurt deeply when my dad was killed. He had been a friend to me, standing up for me and doing little things to keep my courage up. I no longer needed someone to blame. I had someone to trust and that was much better. "I do forgive you."

Porter smiled weakly. "Thank you, Polly," was all he could manage. He took a steadying breath and looked at me. There was a new determination in his expression. "There's one more thing before you go." He looked up past me and nodded. The officer pulled a manila envelope from a briefcase on the floor that I had not noticed before.

"Go and sign it, Polly," Porter instructed. "The deed to the Forgotten Mine is yours. Anything found in the mine is to be used as you and your guardian see fit."

"I'm on there as a guardian until you come of age," Theo announced proudly.

I looked at them, unable to understand. "Why are you giving the mine to me? The treasure is still down there."

"And you know where it is," Porter pointed out. "Use it to make this world a better place."

I didn't move. It was too much to take in.

"Go ahead, Polly. You have my word that this is all above board and legal," Porter assured me. "I have scraped together enough to pay back the money I stole to buy it. I've even had the deed reviewed by a lawyer. The mine was legally sold to me and now I am giving you the deed. I will be out of touch with things for a while. I want you to have it. I want you to have something to look forward to even if you have to do a spell in foster care or something like that. I think your dad was right. You are a special young lady, and I know God has big plans for you."

"You could probably buy the whole Weatherbee Retreat with it since Mr. Blossom will be facing charges of his own," the officer added.

I stood uncertainly.

"It is all ready except for your signature," Theo told me, stepping out of the way.

Looking at each of them to make sure this was not a joke, I moved to the small, wobbly table that was against the wall the officer stood by. I struggled through enough of the confusing legal paper to know it was what they said it was, and carefully put my name on the line the officer pointed out. Theo was grinning like a proud uncle beside me.

"Why didn't you come get West right after he tried to kill Porter?" I asked, sliding the paper to the center of the little table.

"You are an important witness against West, and we could not take a chance of putting you in danger by moving in on them at the retreat." The officer was casually returning the papers to his briefcase. "Besides, you were down in the mine, and we had no way to reach you, or to know if you were okay. Now that you are safe, and West is here in town, I would guess that they have both been arrested by now."

I stood in stunned silence, feeling somehow cheated. How could it all be over? I didn't get to see West or Grandfather arrested. After all I had been through, this stranger in a suit obviously expected me to take his word and move on. "So the guy's story about me running away back at the tracks was part of the plan?" I handed the pen back to the officer.

"They were in charge of getting you to me. They did very well and stuck to the truth." Theo laughed. "Those boys make quite a team. It was all Porter's idea. It was very important to him that you were safe and that he told you himself."

Turning to look at Porter, I saw that his eyes were closed and his brow was creased with a slight frown. Crossing back to the bedside, I gently took his hand.

Porter's eyes fluttered open wearily. I realized too late that I had awakened him. He must have fallen asleep while we were occupied signing the deed.

"Thank you for saving my life, Porter," I whispered, sitting gingerly on the edge of the hospital bed. When I hesitated, Porter squeezed my hand gently. "You can ask me anything, Polly."

"When they let you go, Porter, will you come find me?"

His familiar smile slid into place, and he squeezed my hand again. "I will do everything I can to find you, Polly Hamilton," Porter promised. "That's what secret friends do."

# Chapter 23

"So much has happened since I escaped from West and met Uncle Theo. Porter and I had to testify against Mr. Blossom and West. They both got pretty heavy sentences according to Uncle Theo. West may get the death penalty if they can prove he killed my dad, but he still gets to stay in jail a long time for attempting to kill Porter. Because Porter was involved in criminal activity and was already wanted by the law, he has to do time too. I wish he didn't. Uncle Theo said they would go lighter on him because he helped the police get West, but the sentence Porter got didn't seem light to me.

My suspicions were right, and it turned out that Mr. Blossom was not related to me at all. My mom was summoned to appear before the judge but never showed up. Twice. This, and the fact that she had actually gotten money for me from Mr. Blossom, means she lost her parental rights. I knew it would happen and I can't say I was sorry to lose her. It's taken several months to get all this sorted out, but I'm hoping it will be over soon.

Because I'm a minor, and there were no actual relatives willing to claim me, I'll have to go to a foster home. I should have gone already according to the sour faced lady who knows about these things. I guess Uncle Theo has some connections that go way back. Someone higher up, I think Jake said it was Mayor Easton, let me stay at Uncle Theo's as my temporary foster family until everything was for sure with my mom's rights being terminated. Jake's dad works for the mayor.

Theo and Helen Thimbleton have five kids including Robert. I finally got a clear answer about why he doesn't look like his dad. Robert was adopted when he was nine. He's been a part of the family so long that it's like he has always belonged. I hope that can happen to me some day. I have never been a part of a together family before and am enjoying the experience. Even if it technically made Robert my foster brother."

A gentle breeze pushed my hair out of my face. With a contented sigh, I looked up from my journal. It was a leather bound version like my dad's, only smaller. Martha stopped by and gave it to me before she left town. The Weatherbee Retreat was closed for investigation, so there wouldn't be a job for her there anymore. Everything had changed so fast. Uncle Theo said that everyone in town would have to work a little harder to make ends meet without the retreat to draw the tourists.

I let my eyes wander over the familiar rocky scenery. Even though I had not been here long, somehow it felt like home. Tomorrow they would take me away.

I thought of my dad's journal and I was glad it was in a safe place. When I aged out of the foster system, I would come back for it. Or, if by some miracle, someone wanted to adopt a homely eleven-year-old girl like me, I would convince them to bring me back to get it sooner.

Having settled my plans, I carefully wrapped the leather strap around my journal to keep it shut.

A movement across the rocky field caught my attention. It was Jake, bounding and leaping like a deer across the rough terrain. My smiled faded as he got closer. His face was pale and streaked with sweat and he was shouting something I could not make out.

Instinctively, I looked around for any sign of danger. The field was silent except for Jake's crashing and whatever it was he was hollering. I went toward him, even after several months. I was still pretty unstable if I tried to go fast over the rocks.

"What is it, Jake?" I called.

He slowed slightly, glanced around, and beckoned me to hurry.

I did my best, trying to watch my footing and the on-coming teen at the same time.

"Polly, thank God you are safe. We've got to get out of here!" Jake grabbed my arm and propelled me toward the road. Even though I was stumbling along, his firm grip kept me upright as we closed the distance to the road.

"What happened, Jake?" I demanded, trying hard to keep my footing.

"He's out," Jake answered breathlessly. "Polly, West got out last night."

"Of prison?!" I couldn't believe it. West was supposed to be in prison for years. If Jake had not been all sweaty and pale, I would have laughed it off as a good joke. "How?"

"By killing people." Jake was too busy checking the sur-rounding area and his footing to bother looking at me. "We have to get you somewhere safe."

"Who did he kill?" There was a cold, sick feeling in my stomach now.

"I didn't stay for the details. I think he killed a guard, or maybe more than one, I'm not sure. Uncle Theo called my dad and sent us out to find you. They are sticking to the radios in case more information comes through and serving as a home base for the armed search parties that have been sent out."

My foot missed the rock and I stumbled. I didn't go all of the way down, thanks to Jake's firm hold, but my knee connected solidly with the offending rock. "Where are Robert and Jamal?" I asked, scrambling up again. There wasn't time to think about the pain. I knew that if West found me, my bruises would be the least of my worries.

"Robert is up by the mine shaft. Jamal took the back trail down to the stream. The police are driving the roads looking for any sign of West. I knew you did your journal thing out here, so I came this way."

I marveled at the way he was able to multitask. Not only was he running on and over rocks, keeping me upright, and filling me in on the news, but he was also systematically pushing the call button on his walkie-talkie and scanning the area for danger. The walkie-talkie beeped, and Jake's hold on me loosened.

I guess I marveled too soon because in the next moment, I was flat on my face in the coarse grass.

"Sorry." Jake was pulling me to my feet. "Robert, do you read me? I've got her. Meet me at the tree."

"Isn't that a little vague?" I asked trying to brush myself off.

"Not to him." Jake scanned the tree line before glancing down at me. "Grab your journal. We aren't coming back for it."

Gratefully, I snatched up my journal from the ground where it had fallen. I would have dusted it off, but Jake jerked me forward.

I pulled against him. "What are you trying to do, Jake? Pull my arm off?" I asked in irritation. "You might be part gazelle, but I'm not."

Looking genuinely sorry, Jake let go of my arm. "Your life is in danger, Polly."

I could tell he wasn't exaggerating. "How do you even know he's in this area?" I asked, rubbing my sore arm. "I mean, why would he come back here?"

"Walk and I'll tell you," Jake bargained.

"Only if you don't keep trying to pull my arm off," I

countered.

"Deal. Try to keep your feet under you. It might help." He moved forward, and I had no choice but to catch up with his quick stride.

"The police put out all kinds of notices and stuff on TV and the radio," Jake explained as promised. "For people way out here, they do special ham radio communications, and we have a network of people who spread the news when it is urgent." Jake's radio made a static noise.

He turned it up. "You at the tree?"

"Roger that," Robert's voice was muffled but understandable. "Dad said the road is clear so far. We will have to be quick. I have a feeling he already knows where we will take her."

"You think it is safe?" Jake's eyes never stopped looking for signs of West.

"Jamal's dad is with the police force and the volunteer search parties," Robert responded over the radio. "They haven't seen anything, but there was a guy who ran into West at the gas station on the edge of town, and he's got a black eye and broken nose to show for it. This is our only chance. We can't match him."

"Where exactly are you taking me?" I spotted the trail to the Forgotten Mine shaft up ahead.

"The mine shaft," Jake answered. "It is the only place West can't get to you."

I had not expected the shiver of fear that ran up my spine.

"Look, it's a smooth trail now, Polly. Your life is in danger. You've got to trust me and run."

The trail was anything but smooth, but it was much easier going than navigating the tall grass strewn with rocks and boulders that we had come through. No matter how fast I ran, it seemed like Jake was right on my heels. He lived outside and enjoyed pushing himself to greater physical feats.

I slowed a little, pacing myself. The mine shaft was not

far ahead, and I had no desire to go popping out into the overgrown clearing into West's waiting fist.

Jake touched my shoulder, and I stopped dead in my tracks. Crashing into me, Jake sprawled on the path. He blinked at me in shock for a moment before his grin appeared.

"You've got good breaks," he exclaimed softly.

"Sorry." I grinned as I helped him up.

A bird called nearby, and Jake ducked. I followed his lead, keenly aware that there were no other birds calling.

Jake trilled back, soft and hesitant, like a bird testing the air after a silence.

There was no response. We crept further off of the trail, waiting for some signal only Jake knew.

My heart was pounding in my chest. I tried to regulate my breathing so I could hear better.

There was another bird, a different type than the first. Looking over at Jake, I saw him nod. He moved back onto the trail, another soft trill coming from his lips.

The call was repeated, and Jake beckoned to me. We jogged toward the mine shaft, ready to dive for cover at the slightest sign of danger. Though I wondered what good diving for cover would do us if we came across West.

"When we get to the shaft you are going to have to jump right in."

"That's a long fall," I whispered back.

"I mean in the bucket," he trilled and was silent. The answer came from up ahead. "Robert should have the rope ready and the bucket at the top. Don't hesitate. No matter what happens, get down that mine." He jogged in silence for a few minutes.

"What if he hurts you and Robert?" I asked. We were rounding a bend in the trail. One more curve and we would be at the clearing.

"It doesn't matter, Polly. He might bang us around a little, but we don't have anything to make it worthwhile. He must have found out you have the deed to the mine."

"How would he find that out?" I was skeptical.

"I know," Jake pointed out.

I fell silent. Of course West would know by now. Uncle Theo always said, "Small town news spreads faster than soft butter on bread."

"Hurry!" Robert's soft call held a note of urgency.

"Just jump in the hole." I repeated to Jake.

He nodded, looking grim.

Dashing across the open area, I sat on the edge of the shaft and put my feet down into the tight space of the bucket. It seemed tighter now. In that moment, I could understand Jake's fear of tight spaces. Swallowing my fear, I steadied myself on the edges of the narrow shaft.

Robert had the rope, and he immediately started lowering me downward.

Jake grabbed on to the rope, and the bucket dropped faster.

Standing up in the bucket, I gave them a little salute as I sank into the shaft. Jake's smile was one of relief.

"I dropped supplies with your little string when I first got here," Robert told me. "It was all I had on hand." His eyes moved to something on the far side of the clearing, and there was fear in them when he looked back at me. Grabbing something from his back pocket, he dropped to his stomach and thrust down toward me. Standing on my toes to reach, I took the sturdy pocket knife he held out to me and shoved it into my own back pocket.

"In case you have to cut the rope." I could see the fear in his eyes and somehow knew he had seen West.

# Chapter 24

Squirming through the tight spot, I felt the bucket dropping even faster. I wanted to put my hands out to steady myself, instead I pulled the pocket knife from my pocked and flicked it open with one hand like Robert had taught me. With the other hand, I clung to the rope.

"Get her out of there." West's voice boomed across the clearing, sending a wave of terror over me. I knew what he had done to my dad and Porter. And I knew the guys up there were no match for a seasoned killer like West.

I put the blade of the knife against the rope. I could hear a struggle above. The bucket stopped going down. Without giving myself time to think, I braced my back against one side of the shaft wall and my foot against the other side, and cut the rope. The blade was sharp and sliced through the thick rope with very little effort. The bucket fell with a loud, echoing clang. Everything was silent above me. Whoever had been holding the rope, released it. The rope zipped by, stretching out to its full length. It hung there, wavering as if trembling against me. Bracing with any part of my body that would help, I worked my way downward. I knew there was at least six or so feet of shaft beneath me before I would reach the floor of the mine.

A light clicked on above me, shining into my face. I was far enough down to be safe, but not out of reach of his flashlight beam. "Polly, you get up here, now!" West commanded loudly.

Choosing not to answer, I continued my descent.

"If you don't, these boys will meet the same fate your precious father did."

I hesitated, looking up into his flashlight beam. "You won't get anything but more prison time if you kill them," I shouted up.

"I won't lose anything either," West's voice was hard and deadly. "But I believe you might find it hard to live with the knowledge that you were the reason for their deaths. Come up, and I'll let one of them go."

"Look, I don't want the treasure anyway," I called up to him. "The coins are under the kitchen stairs at the retreat. You can have them."

"Only a fool would settle for those measly coins when there is more to be had. I have wasted too much time to take so little payment."

"That's all the treasure I have." My legs were getting tired. "The police are everywhere tracking you down. Get it and leave."

"You think it is that easy?" West growled. "I'm not about to let Porter cross me and walk away. He's not getting this treasure."

"He didn't walk away," I reminded him. "Porter is in jail." If I could stall West long enough, the police might find us and be able to arrest him.

"I said come up." West was pacing by the shaft. I could see his silhouette block the light as he passed.

"Where are the guys?" I demanded. "How do I know you haven't already killed them?"

"Nice try. If they make so much as a peep, I'll shoot down the shaft." West laughed cruelly. "Seems like I have something each party cares about. Which means that I have the upper hand."

"So what do you want?" I was creeping downward whenever he passed the shaft, and I knew his back was to me. "Even if I come up, what good will it do you?" I really wanted to know.

"You will get me the treasure, and you will help me get past the police. Nobody actually wants you, Polly. You might as well admit it. Even your dad didn't want you. He said so."

I wasn't looking up so he did not see me smile. A year ago I would have believed him. I would have been torn up inside by the awful lie. Not anymore. I had read enough of Dad's journal to know the truth, and it turns out that the truth really does set people free.

"If I come up, you will let one of the guys go?" I asked, pausing my descent.

West stopped pacing and shone the light into my face once more. "You have my word of honor."

"That means absolutely nothing to me," I answered. "You let one guy go if I come up, but what about the other guy? I'm guessing you will trade him for access to the tunnel?"

"Right again."

I thought for a moment. "After you get in and get what you want, you will clear out?"

"What reason would I have to stay?" I could hear the eagerness in his voice.

"And you will leave me here?"

"You may buy your freedom by giving me the treasure."

"Okay. I'll grab the rope. You pull me up."

West laughed, "Nice try. I'll have these idle boys pull you up. My hands seem to be full at the moment."

Grabbing onto the rope, I hung on tightly. "I'm waiting."

"Pull her up, and no funny business," West commanded. "I have you both covered."

The rope started moving upward. I could tell by the speed that they, too, were hoping for a miracle. West was growing impatient, and I knew that once he got angry, he threw off all self-control.

"Hurry up, Robert," I called up to them. I got through the tight spot, and West grabbed my wrist, jerking me up with surprising strength.

Robert and Jake stood looking at me with disappointment and a hint of anger.

"Alright, one guy goes free," I reminded West, masking my fear.

"Polly, why?" Robert breathed softly.

"I choose the talkative one," West's grin was cruel. "Get lost." His eyes met Robert's with a hard gleam.

"I'm not going anywhere," Robert answered bravely.

"Robert, you have to," I pleaded. "I need you to go. You are like a brother to me. I need you to be okay."

"And leave you here?" Robert gestured at West, "With him? Are you out of your mind?"

"You can't help me here," I hoped he would understand.

Robert glared at West, his teeth clenched. "You haven't won this." He turned and started walking back toward the trail.

A sound behind me seemed to stop time.

Robert turned slightly, his face registering shock as he sank to the ground.

"You said he would go free!" I screamed in anger. "You gave me your worthless word of honor." I wanted to hurt him, to get even any way I could. Grabbing madly at clods of dirt and small rocks I blindly pelted West with them, yelling every insult I could think of.

Something hit me, knocking me to the ground. I struggled to catch my breath as I stared up at West's angry face above me.

"You stop that," he boomed.

I looked over where Robert lay. It was my fault. I thought of Uncle Theo and of all the pain I had caused.

"It was a tranquilizer," Jake's brief statement broke through my grief.

"You stay out of this!" West grabbed him by the front of his shirt.

Jake wisely held his tongue and did not fight back.

"You said he could go free," I was on my feet again. My hand trembled as I pointed at Robert's body. "You promised he could go free if I came up."

"Children are so emotional," West spat distastefully, his anger seemed to be passing. "I said he could go free, and he will…once he wakes up." He was the only one who found his little trick amusing.

"Shall we move on to the second part of your bargain?"

"I give you the entrance to the mine for him?" I verified motioning at Jake. "Or at least a tranquilized version of him?"

West smirked. "You catch on fast."

"You had no reason to do that to Robert." I walked toward where Robert lay and West grabbed my arm roughly.

"I'm not moving on until I know you kept this part of the deal." Jerking my arm out of his grasp, I met his look with a fierce one of my own. "Take it or leave it." I put my fists on my hips and waited.

"She's a feisty little kitten, isn't she?" West mocked. "Go check him if you must. You have one minute. I would hate to get my guns mixed up and miss out on the rest of our partnership."

"Sure you would," I muttered. The fear I had felt before was completely gone. I checked how Jamal had showed me, and Robert's pulse was strong beneath my fingers.

I stood and faced West. "Okay, phase two. Take me to the retreat."

He looked irritated. "That slippery eel was doing it right under our noses."

Wanting to make a snide remark about calling my dad names, I pressed my lips together to keep it inside. There was no reason to taunt an angry bear, especially if it was doing what you wanted. If I could get West to the retreat, I knew that there would be officers there. There was always one stationed in a car at the driveway to keep snoopy locals out. I needed to get the real gun from West. He had killed enough that a few more lives would mean nothing to him. Once he was in the mine, he would have less space to maneuver. It would be he and I then. Jake would get tranquilized at the entrance to the mine. That is, if West kept his word again which seemed more and more unlikely.

"Don't think too much, kid," West warned darkly.

Realizing I had been frowning, I looked at him expectantly. "It is a long walk to the retreat. Hadn't we better start?"

He eyed me suspiciously. We were caught in a tense game of life and death which teetered precariously on a thin line of trust. A trust neither of us had any faith in.

Praying silently, I followed West's direction to take the path Porter and I had used so long ago to get to the mine shaft. It puzzled me because the trip had taken Porter and I over an hour on a 4 wheeler. Now West, a wanted criminal, was casually strolling behind me as if he had all the time in the world. Between West and me, Jake walked silently. I wondered what he could be thinking. I had totally disregarded their attempt at protection. Not because I didn't appreciate it, but because I knew West would kill them as heartlessly as he had the others in order to get what he wanted.

"Through here."

I looked back to see West pointing at a thin path that cut off of the main trail. I had always thought Grandfather had dropped him off. This trail could have been how he met us so promptly at the mine the day he tried to kill Porter.

Following the trail he had pointed out, we walked straight ahead for several minutes. The trail shifted left or right, but it never turned. It was as if someone were using a compass and adjusting each time they checked their bearings. Now and then we would cross the wider trail as it wove its way across the uneven terrain.

"Get down!" West hissed, and we obeyed. Two men on four wheelers passed not far from us.

"Speed up." He commanded once the coast was clear. "If I don't get what I want, you lose everything."

I nodded and started jogging. I could hear the other two behind me. It wasn't long before West's breathing became heavy. Without glancing back I slowed slightly. Jake followed my lead, slowly decreasing the pace until we were walking quickly again. West made no comment. After several minutes his breathing returned to normal.

The trail readjusted several more times, and we crouched and hid as a few more members of the search party passed. I stole a glance back and saw West was sweating. He looked nervous. This meant I would have to be more careful not to trigger his anger. Scared, angry people are more likely to act from of their emotion instead of their brains. I knew that from experience.

"Go," West hissed once the patrol had passed. "You had better be leading me to that entrance. I'm holding a real gun, and if anything looks wrong, this guy will take the hit."

"I'm leading you to it," I assured him calmly.

He narrowed his eyes and jerked his chin toward the path, "Get going."

We walked on and on. There was no sound from Jake besides the crunching of his shoes on the trail. I wondered what time it was. The sun was still on the way up. I had been in the field around 9 am.

"Stop here." West's command interrupted my thoughts.

I looked around and saw the tall roof of the retreat over the trees. "It's in the garden."

He studied me distrustfully, "You better not be leading

me into a trap."

"You have my word, which actually does mean something," I informed him. "If you let Jake go, I will show you the entrance."

"I'll let him go when you show me the entrance," West corrected, emphasizing the word when.

"Right. What is the quickest, safest way to the garden?"

For a moment, he looked undecided, but he knew as well as I did that he could not afford to waste time. "Go left and keep inside the tree line."

I nodded and started walking. I wanted to look at Jake, to see how he was taking it all, but I didn't dare. The tree line thinned, and I stopped. Across a patch of grass that needed to be mowed was the first hedges of the garden. I looked over at West for direction. Jake's head was down, so I could not see his face. He had been walking for what seemed like hours with a gun at his back.

Moving past us to the edge of the tree line, West peered out over the lawn. Time stretched on silently. A stealthy mission like this seemed out of place in the broad daylight.

Finally, West nodded and moved away from us to cross the open lawn.

In that split second I looked at Jake. "Run now."

He opened his mouth to protest, but I shook my head. "I gave my word." Hurrying after West I was with him before he rounded the hedge.

"Where is he?" West demanded angrily shoving the gun at me.

"Kill me now and you will have nothing," I told him softly. "I gave you my word. I will show you the entrance."

For an instant, he seemed surprised. Regaining his rough composure, West growled. "Then where is it?"

"In the fountain."

His brow creased slightly. "He was a clever fox," he murmured to himself. "If only he had not been so stubborn."

"It wasn't about the entrance of the mine was it?"

He looked at me sharply.

"The argument you had before you beat him up, it wasn't about the mine at all, was it?"

A dark look that scared me came into his face. "That is my business. Show me the entrance."

"The mine is dangerous," I had to warn him.

The dark look had not lifted. When he spoke, it was through clenched teeth. "The entrance."

I nodded. Crouching over, I ran along the hedge, knowing it would be hard for West to keep up. I lengthened the distance between us, ducking around hedges like a wild rabbit as I worked my way to the fountain. When I arrived, I saw no sign of West. Opening the panel and the secret hatch, I hesitated looking into the blackness of the tunnel entrance. I wanted more than anything to go inside the mine and get Dad's journal. I was so close. A twig snapped, and I knew I could not risk it. I could hear West's winded breathing coming my way through the last hedge row. He would find the opening which meant that I had fulfilled my portion of the bargain for Jake's life. Putting the fountain between us, I ran back into the garden, dodging and weaving through the untrimmed plants. There was a stretch of open grass before I would be safely back in the woods. I hesitated on the edge of it. If West was looking for me, at this distance he could easily pick me off with his gun as I ran. Again a twig snapped, and I spun around. Jamal grinned at me and put a finger to his lips. He held a broken twig in his hand.

Beckoning to me, he pointed out a deeply shaded alcove between the hedge and a low hanging tree. I wriggled my way through what looked like a little tunnel under the hedge and scooted over as he squirmed in beside me. We sat side by side with our knees drawn up in front of us. I hugged my knees close, waiting. West could not afford to rage or call. Even shooting would alert the police. He had the entrance but nothing else. I had given him what I agreed to and nothing more.

"How did you find me?"

Jamal had to tilt his head to hear me. When I softly repeated my question, he grinned and tapped his temple wisely.

"You knew were the entrance was."

He shook his head no, and put his finger to his lips.

I made a face at him, and he grinned again.

We waited for what seemed forever. There was no sound from the garden or anywhere else.

Jamal's elbow touched mine, and I looked up. A little rabbit was coming tentatively toward us as if wondering at our presence in his secret place.

It was nice to see something normal. Laying my head on my knees, I watched the rabbit go about its business. It was peaceful, and I felt myself relax a little.

# Chapter 25

I woke up to Jamal shaking me and calling my name. I lifted my head, blinking to clear my eyes.

"Don't we have to be quiet?" I asked, not bothering to whisper. He wasn't being quiet anymore.

"Nope. We are safe." He shook his head, grinning at me.

"Why are you staring at me?" I asked groggily. "Is my hair that crazy?"

He laughed, "To be honest, it is a little wild. I just can't figure you. You are just a kid and somehow you are as tough as a wolverine."

I couldn't help smiling. "I'm guessing that's a compliment."

Jamal just shook his head, "You saved so many lives today, Polly Hamilton. We don't actually know how many because if there had been a showdown between West and the police, more people would have died."

"Did they catch West?" I rubbed my eyes to clear them.

"He went in the mine." Jamal wasn't looking at me.

I frowned. "So did I. That doesn't mean he's not going to come out again."

His face changed. "They think he fell. Not long after you fell asleep, the police discovered the secret entrance."

"With your help?" I grinned knowingly.

"I could have had something to do with it." Jamal's face grew animated. "Do you know how high that fountain can spray? I will have to show you some day. It is impressive."

"What happened after the police came?" I prompted.

"It sounded like West knew he was done and tried to make a run for it deeper into the mine. They heard him yell and couldn't get any response from him after that."

"He fell into the path." Remembering the gaping holes in the path just before I reached the entrance, I shuddered to think of the terror of falling through one into the inky blackness.

"Into the path?" Jamal looked confused.

"It isn't nice to think about," I told him.

"Okay, let's not think about it yet." Jamal flattened himself onto his stomach and started to move out under the hedge, still talking as he went. "First, we get out of this tiny little nature space. Then the investigators were wondering if you would be willing to help them out. You know the mine and could show them where the dangerous bits are."

Following him out into the sunlight, I blinked at the crowd that was gathered around. A few news reporters snapped pictures from a polite distance. Jamal's dad had me sit in the long grass while he checked my vitals and asked me a bunch of questions. Once he gave the all clear, a graying man in a sharp suit came over to shake my hand. He said a lot of words, but it was hard for me to follow. At some points, I couldn't tell if he was talking to me or the camera men standing around, so I did my best to look pleasant. Jamal, at my elbow, brought me up to speed with a quick, "That's the mayor. He says, 'Thank you.'"

"My hair is still a mess." I told him out of the side of my mouth. "Now the whole world will see it."

"Your face is all smudgy too." Grinning, Jamal leaned closer. "Don't worry. My dad says it keeps a body humble to look off their game now and then. Just don't make a habit of it, or they think you don't care."

I shoved him away. "Go find Robert." Realizing what

I said, I left the Mayor to finish his long speech about the safety of the town being first priority and made my way over to Jamal's dad.

"Excuse me?"

He looked down at me in surprise and then looked over to where the Mayor had just noticed I was gone.

I didn't care about the Mayor anymore. "Do you know where Robert is?"

His grin was just like Jamal's. "I was thinking that might come up. He's drowsy but awake. We went ahead and sent him in to the hospital to be monitored to make sure there are no side effects. Not sure what type of tranquilizer he was hit with. In fact, we aren't even sure how West got his hands on it. Jake made it to Old Mr. Johnson's place and radioed out the news. The ambulance team was sent to pick up Robert, and I came on over here to see if I could help on this side. Jamal had that fountain going sky high so it didn't take much to get the police in the right place. I was sorry West had to go the way he did, but God's justice is often more merciful than man's." He looked down at me and smiled. "I don't have much experience with girls, but I would guess even a little thing like you would be hungry by now."

I had not thought about it until then, but at the mention of food, I was definitely hungry. "Do you think the police would mind if I got something to eat before we go into the mine?"

He crinkled his nose and shook his head. "If they do, they will have to get over it. I'm officially prescribing it, so we are getting you something to eat." He looked around and gave a little whistle. Jamal came trotting over to where we stood. "We are going to get us something to eat. You want something?"

"Finally! I thought I would have to shrivel up like a raisin before someone noticed."

"You would have to wait a long time for something like that to happen to you, Son." He laughed, slapping Jamal on the shoulder. "But this little girl might blow away if we don't get something in her to weigh her down."

It was fun to laugh.

Jamal's dad cleared our errand with the police, and before I realized it, we were standing at the steps by the kitchen porch. The steps my dad had made.

"You okay?" Jamal asked pausing part way up the steps.

"I thought the house was closed up."

"It was, but the police needed somewhere to put their headquarters, and this was close," Jamal explained. "Dad told me."

"I found some of the treasure in the mine."

Jamal's face lit up with interest. "Yeah?"

"I hid it in these stairs."

"There's something else in the stairs. If you are going back in the mine, it is time you knew."

I frowned, not understanding.

"Come on. I'll show you." He led the way down the steps, and we crouched to crawl under the porch. He looked at me, seeming somehow older, and pointed at the flat backside of the steps. "Where did you hide it?"

I pressed on the end of the brick, and it slid out a little. "In there."

"Did it not strike you as odd that the brick came out?" He asked.

"I did think about it later, but I couldn't ever get back to look at it." I pulled the brick out and took the coins from the hollowed crevice inside.

"There's one more thing in there." Jamal was watching me with a twinkle of excitement in his eyes.

"How…?" I put my hand in and felt a piece of thick paper. Pulling it out, I realized it was almost identical to the folded paper I had found in the Forgotten Mine under the treasure box. The markings were the same, all in a perfectly straight line, but not making any more sense than the ones on the first paper.

"How did you know this was here?"

"I knew your dad, Polly," Jamal answered seriously. "He was a good friend of mine. Mason knew something bad was going to happen. He had told the sergeant in town and was getting ready to move on. He said the treasure hunt was not worth his life. He was set on finding you Polly and letting you know how much he cared about you."

I toyed with the coins, waiting for him to go on.

"He had already packed and said goodbye to me the day before. Mr. Blossom wanted him to seal up the mine shaft before he left so it would not be a hazard on his property. Your dad told me about this because he knew how much Mr. Blossom wanted that treasure. It did not make sense to seal the shaft when it was the only way into the mine that they knew about. Your dad was afraid they would try something once he got to the mine and wanted someone he could trust to know about the clue. That was why he was out there when West met him by the shaft." Jamal was not looking at me as he spoke. He was staring off into the dim crawlspace under the house. Some memories hurt more when they are brought into the light, but often there cannot be healing until they are. "I don't know what happened out there," he continued. "I guess you can imagine how much I wished I had been there to help your dad like you did Porter. People say West was trying to get Mason to tell where the entrance to the mine was. I think West was actually trying to force your dad to stay. He got angry and flew off the handle, did more damage than he meant to, and staged your dad's death. There was no way to prove it, but I always knew it was not really an accident." He sighed and looked at me. "And that brings us to today.

Your dad told me about the hidden clue when he decided to go. He said I was to keep it a secret until it was needed. He had a lot of faith in me, me being a teen boy and all. He always said I didn't have to be a dumb teen like the world expected. I could skip that and become a respected man any time I chose." He smiled at me. "By the way you live, I think he must have told you some similar things growing up. You are unbelievably mature for an 11 year old."

"Thanks." I didn't know what else to say.

"And I thought you two were hungry." Jamal's dad had stooped to see where we had gone and stood there, shaking his head at us. "I got all that food ready and here you sit in the dirt just chatting away."

We crawled out, both doing our best to convince him that we really were famished.

"I guess I'll just have to throw out all that food I made," he said sadly.

"You made?"

My eyes lit up at the sound of Mrs. Ella's voice. I spun to see her standing on the top step, just like she had so many times before. I ran up and hugged her tightly. She hugged me back. Laughing she stepped back to look at me.

"Polly, you are a mess! Your face is filthy. Go wash up, and I'll have your food ready when you come out." I gave her another quick hug before running inside. I didn't think I could be happier until I saw Martha step out of the laundry room.

Up to now, I had not been the hugging type. Now I found I had so many people that I truly cared about.

"Martha!"

She grinned and held open her arms. I hugged her tightly.

She looked down at me, her hair as wild as ever. "Good to see you, Polly. I came with Miss Ella as soon as we heard you were in danger. Speaking of Miss Ella, we'd better get you washed up." She turned, putting her arm around my shoulder as we walked to the sink together.

"Martha, I'm going to use that treasure and buy this retreat. The whole thing."

She laughed happily at the thought. "If anyone could, Polly, it would be you."

"If I do, will you work here? I want to give kids who have been passed around a place to enjoy life. We can do the tourist season still to get money and all that, but I want to use it in the off-season too. To help families who are helping kids like me. Would you work here if I did all that?"

She held out a washcloth to me. "Polly Hamilton, I would be honored to work for you."

# Chapter 26

"You aren't all going to fit down there," I told the group of police waiting by the mine entrance. I could tell they all wanted to go in.

"I'll make it into a tour," I told Jake who was standing beside me. "I'll charge admission and everything."

"You will have to get the treasure before you start spending it," Jamal reminded me.

"What are we waiting for?" an officer asked, looking around.

"Polly has requested we allow her, Robert, Jake, and Jamal a chance to crack the mystery of her dad's codes before we all go piling in haphazardly." The inspector responded with a wink at me. He was a tall thin man with a dry sense of humor. I had liked him at once. I had gone in with a few special officers three days ago, when West had disappeared. That's when I had retrieved Dad's journal from the crevice where it had been hidden. It was still dry and safe even after so much time had passed. Surfacing again, the inspector's man had copied down the symbols Dad had made to keep people safe in the mine. They had also confirmed that West had fallen through the gaping hole in the path in his attempt to escape from the police. Experts had come and taken his body to be buried.

In a way, I was sad he had not had to pay for his wrongs. I mentioned it to Uncle Theo, and he reminded me that in heaven people are judged for what they do here. He said that God is merciful but He is also just. Those who trust Him here, will receive His mercy. Those who reject Him here on earth will receive only His justice. I think it would be terrifying to die and have to face the punishment for all your sins just because you were proud and wanted to have your own way during your short lifetime here.

"Here he is!"

I looked up from my musings to see Robert coming toward us.

"He's alive!" Jake greeted him with an enthusiastic hug. I could tell he was a little emotional. The last time we had seen him, Robert was lying on the ground looking dead. Once the handshakes, fist bumps, and hugs were over, we turned our attention to the mine.

"Remember, you all are only to go down to the first tunnel. No heroics down there. You are not to go past what you call the 'Swiss Cheese' part of the trail. We have it clearly marked off. Are we agreed?" The inspector looked me in the eyes, and it felt like he was reading my mind.

"Yes, Sir. We will figure out the clues and let you know when we are ready."

He nodded, satisfied. "Let us know if you need any help."

We scrambled into the narrow entrance and down the trap door. Jake was sweating profusely by the time we got into the tunnel.

"Does it get any wider?" he asked nervously.

I remembered how I had felt going back into the mine. "Yes, keep your light on the floor. There's caution tape up a little ways before the holes in the path, but you don't want to get too close."

"Anywhere there's more space is great with me." He walked a little ways from the stairs and sighed with relief as the tunnel widened.

"Do you have the clues?" Jamal asked.

"Right here. I opened my dad's journal and pulled out the two pieces. "This one I've looked over so many times. And this one…" I separated the papers, "this one is the new one Jamal knew about."

"How did Jamal know about it?" Jake asked from a distance.

"You can ask him about all that later. Do you guys have any ideas?" I spread the two pieces on the stone floor. Both were double sided and had a single line of gibberish on each side.

Robert picked up one of the papers to examine it closer with his flashlight. "It is almost English. I can see some similarities in the letters, but at the same time, it's not."

Jamal scrunched his eyes to see if that revealed anything new.

Jake was inching closer.

"You have any ideas, Jake?" I asked, moving aside.

He looked for a moment, thoughtfully. "It's a spineless book. I saw it in an old spy book about codes I got for Christmas."

We all looked at him.

It seemed he had forgotten about the tight space in his excitement. He came forward and took the paper from Robert. Folding it in half lengthwise along the middle of the line of text, he put it on the floor. Only the top half of the line of symbols was visible. Folding the other paper in half the same way, he laid it below the first paper so the two folds were touching one above the other. We shone our lights while he worked, but the end result was another line of gibberish.

Robert's eyes lit up, "I get it!"

He and Jake swapped the papers. Jake folded the top one the opposite way, and then Robert flipped his.

"That's it!" Jake exclaimed.

We all crowded in to look. He was right, the odd symbols I had been trying to decipher were partial letters, letters completed by the other half of the odd symbols on the new paper.

"What does it say?" Jamal asked, adding the beam of his flashlight.

"Invest with care." Jake looked at us to see if it meant more to anyone else than it did to him.

"I think it is a message about how to use the treasure." Robert was serious.

Looking over at him I nodded. We both knew that using the treasure wisely would be an important task.

"Let's see the other side. Maybe that's only part of the message," Jake pointed out. He turned both pieces over the same direction and read, "fragrant entranc." He looked at me, "It is spelled wrong," he pointed out. "There's no E." Remembering my dad had written it, Jake added, "Don't worry about it. Spelling can be hard."

"Mason knew how to spell, Jake. It had to match the length of the other lines." Jamal laughed. "Do you know where the fragrant entrance is, Polly?"

"I only know of this entrance." Looking away, I searched for a faint memory that was tugging at my mind. "I do remember that when I came up, I smelled the garden before I saw it. It makes sense. The garden would make this entrance fragrant because the flowers smell nice."

"Hang on. There's more." Robert had unfolded one of the papers and refolded it the opposite direction on the same seam.

We looked, but none of us could make out any words. Jamal reached over and refolded the other piece and we laughed, relieved to see words once more.

"Under two of three," I read. "That's not super helpful," I observed for us all.

"When you were down here before, Polly, did you see three of anything anywhere?" Jake asked.

I thought for a minute, but nothing came to mind. Shaking my head, I flipped over both papers to reveal the 4th line of the book without a binding.

"Structure unharmed," Robert read aloud for us all. "So we have, structure unharmed, under two of three, fragrant entrance, and invest wisely."

I looked around the passage. Further on were the dangerous holes that dropped away into the depth of the mine. There were more than three holes, so that couldn't be it. Back the way we had come, the tunnel narrowed to the place where three steps led up to the trap door.

"Two of three! It's the second step!" I exclaimed with a thrill of excitement, scrambling to my feet. "If you remove the center brick, it's like the game, Jenga, the structure will be unharmed. Come on!"

Jake, caught up in the thrill of discovery, forgot his fear of small spaces. That is until he stopped suddenly in front of me, and I crashed into the back of him.

"What's wrong?" I asked looking past him and seeing nothing.

"You all go on ahead," he stepped aside, wiping sweat from his face. "This tunnel is getting a little tight with all of us going to the narrowest point. I'm hoping it's the narrowest point." He muttered the last part to himself.

"Everything okay?" Jamal and Robert had picked up the papers in case they were needed later.

"I think Polly should get to look. She found the entrance," Jake told them bravely.

"Good point. Polly, it is all yours." Robert gave me a bold, sweeping bow.

Jamal grinned, "Go ahead, Polly." He knew the secret of the other steps and could have easily found whatever was hidden here. I smiled my thanks.

Moving past them, I examined the steps. One side faced us, and the other was up against the end of the man-made tunnel.

"Do you think we have to have some kind of tool to break into them?" Robert asked peering over me at the steps.

"No, Dad was too proud of his work to have someone destroy it." I moved closer, running my fingers over the bricks that made up the middle step. It was made up of four bricks across and three high. I pressed on the small end of the center brick, and it slid out about an inch when I stopped pushing.

"I found it!"

Pulling out the brick, I saw it was like the secret brick under the kitchen stair. It too had been hollowed out like a tiny drawer. "Here it is!" I held up the paper folded inside.

For Jake's sake, we moved back to the open end of the tunnel before unfolding the new clue. Spreading the paper out on the stone floor, Robert stood above us and held his flashlight so we could all see by its light.

"It's a map." Jamal knelt to trace the passageway with his finger. "There's the Swiss cheese part where West fell." He shone his light down the tunnel into the darkness. The treacherous holes in the path were out of the reach of his beam.

Robert crouched and tapped the paper. "There's the X."

He was right. A dark X marked the map. I cocked my head trying to remember the actual caverns I had passed through. The tunnels ran like a maze crisscrossing as they went.

Sitting back on my heels, I looked at my fellow treasure hunters. "Shall we call the inspector?"

They grinned back at me. "It is time to find that treasure!"

# Chapter 27

"It is hard to believe that eight years have passed since we found the second treasure down in the mine. It was a one of the largest stashes of civil war coins to be discovered. It was worth more than enough to accomplish what I had envisioned back when I was eleven. In fact, as I write this, I'm sitting up on my favorite mountain outlook over the Weatherbee Mine. I can see almost all the property around the retreat's main lodge. It is still strange to think it all belongs to me now. Originally, Uncle Theo and I had to purchase it together because I was still a minor. Now that I'm 19, it has belonged to me for over a year. Of course, I could never keep it going by myself.

The perfectly manicured garden is Uncle Theo's and Aunt Helen's pride and joy. Robert is the mechanic and keeps all the tourist's rental vehicles running smoothly. Those machines endure a lot of abuse on the trails. We have had most of the touring trails smoothed out which has helped with safety as well as upkeep. Robert is married now, and has a little guy of his own. It won't be long before little Robby can ride with his dad, leading the trail tours for our guests.

Martha is still on staff and is training Mattie, one of Uncle Theo's girls, to take her place someday as head of hospitality. We have a full-time team for hospitality now that the retreat is active all year round. Miss Ella has several full time cooks under her as well. We joke that the steady flow of guests is only because of her good cooking.

Jamal's dad retires next year from work as an EMT, and Jamal is quickly rising in the ranks. It has been several months since his marriage to Kim. I don't think I have ever seen him as happy as when he is with her. They both wear those sharp looking EMT uniforms he always wanted to have. During the tourist season, they stay around the retreat to help with any injuries. We provide first aid training and three levels of biking classes for the tourists and foster families who come to our retreat. Those are the hands on classes Jamal and Robert enjoy teaching. Jake likes to jump in on the action when he can.

When Jake went away to school to become an accountant, he had big ideas about traveling the world, but a young lady going through law school changed all that. After he finished his degree, they decided to settle down here in his home town. Always quick to learn, Jake has shown himself to be quite handy under Porter's direction. I don't think there could be a better teacher than Porter. Together, they run the Weatherbee Retreat with precision while still preserving its charm.

Speaking of Porter, it is so good to have him back. He got out of prison before I turned 18, and he kept his promise to come find me. Uncle Theo doesn't enjoy the managing side of things and was glad to bring Porter on staff again. Porter is like a dad to me. He loves the Lord deeply, and I can always go to him when I need to talk something through.

I get encouragement from my dad too. Over the years, I read his journal so much that now it is practically falling apart. I have put it on display in the little Forgotten Mine Museum we set up. It helps me remember how far God has brought me, and the influence one person can have on so many lives around them. I don't even have to open it since I have most of it memorized.

Over the years, we have made some updates to the old retreat building, but we were careful to preserve the retreat's old, homey feel. Last year, Porter convinced me to write out *the story of the Forgotten Mine. Now the book is for sale in our gift shop. I titled it, The Forgotten Mine."*

With a contented sigh, I closed my journal. Looking out over the vast expanse beneath me, I thought of the last line of *The Forgotten Mine*: The world saw Polly's treasure as the gold and silver found in the forgotten mine, but in her eyes the true treasure is the family she had gained.

## STRENGTH OF SILENCE

Eddie stayed where he was, listening. In the distance, a motor started up. He waited until it had faded before he stood. Dizziness washed over him, and he steadied himself against the counter. Still moving unsteadily, Eddie removed the floorboards and laid them aside. He heard something out front and froze. If the police caught him here, there would be no end of trouble. Moving toward the back door Eddie pushed it open. Outside, trash cans and a variety of other things littered the yard. A car motor rumbled toward him, and Eddie ran.

## JASON ROPER

Infused with invincibility and trained for greatness, Jason Roper is set to fulfill his father's dreams. But when Roper deviates from the instructions he is given, he stumbles upon an expansive criminal network. Determined to use his power to help those in need, Jason Roper discovers that there are times when invincibility alone is not enough.

Is Jason Roper destined for greatness as he has been told, or is his life just a front for a larger, more sinister plan?

# ROPER RETURNS

Jason Roper's second mission is clear-cut. He moves in with confidence, feeling invincible and unstoppable. But things are not what they appear on the surface. Even his invincibility has limits Roper did not know.

With no one to turn to, Roper finds himself sinking into a darkness he does not have the power to evade.

---

## THE MAN BEHIND THE MELODY

The unexpected death of his twin sister threw Mark into a whirlwind of change. Disowned by his stepfather, Mark set out with only one goal in mind, to get as far away from the hateful man as possible. He clung desperately to the last link with his sister, her saxophone. Wandering the streets, Mark's path crossed with a stranger who could see potential no one else could see. Mark, an unwanted orphan, was offered the chance to become more than he had ever dreamed. But could the stranger be trusted?

# CARBON
## AN UNFORGETTABLE ADVENTURE

Carbon slipped out of bed and turned on the light. Taking a sheet of thick drawing paper from her desk she drew the face of the man the article simply called Roper. Pulling the picture she had drawn earlier from her file box, she laid them side by side on the desk. It was little or nothing to go on. The prisoner could have been a thousand different people. She had no face to compare. Suddenly the image of the stranger in the alley came to mind and Carbon frowned thoughtfully. He was the only one who would know.

# ROPER

Protecting his family was Jason Roper's top priority. When his identity is exposed by a bullet that should have taken his life, Roper scrambles to try to protect the ones he loves most. Only this time, it is him they are after.

# IN VISIBLE FEAR

Billy dropped back on the bed, flickering between the visible world and the invisible. His breathing was rapid and irregular.

"Keep quiet, Billy, and I'll do my best to keep them off your trail. They were asking about you today."

"Don't let them find me." Again, Billy grasped the man's shirt, terror in his eyes.

The dark man pried his fingers open and stepped away. "You keep your mouth shut, I'll do what I can."

## Just Ordinary
### And Other Stories

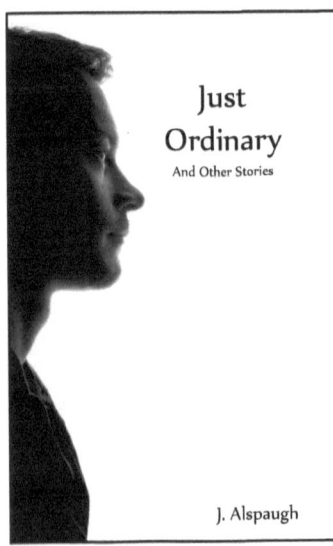

Is there anyone who is truly just ordinary? Step into the world of fiction where heroes face mythical enemies, wrestle against enticing deceit, and battle fierce storms in a struggle for life. Experience heartbreak, adventure, and the ultimate sacrifice as you delve into the stories of *Just Ordinary*.

# THE STRIKER OF CHOI

The health of the Striker is the health of Choi. If he goes hungry, the town of Choi will grow hungry. If he is injured, the townspeople will suffer injury. He must be protected at all costs and must never leave the town of his birth. If he were to leave, the curse of the town would be in the hands of strangers.

Striker knew the legend well, but was there more to the legend than he had been told?

# THE SWORD OF JUSTICE

His mission was to eliminate those who had received the death penalty from the king. Justice was a King's Man. A man who had sworn allegiance to the king and who was backed in power by the full authority of the king himself. A man hated by every criminal in the king's realm.

Would Justice's loyalty to the king and skill with a sword be enough to protect him from his enemies?